Dancing Queen

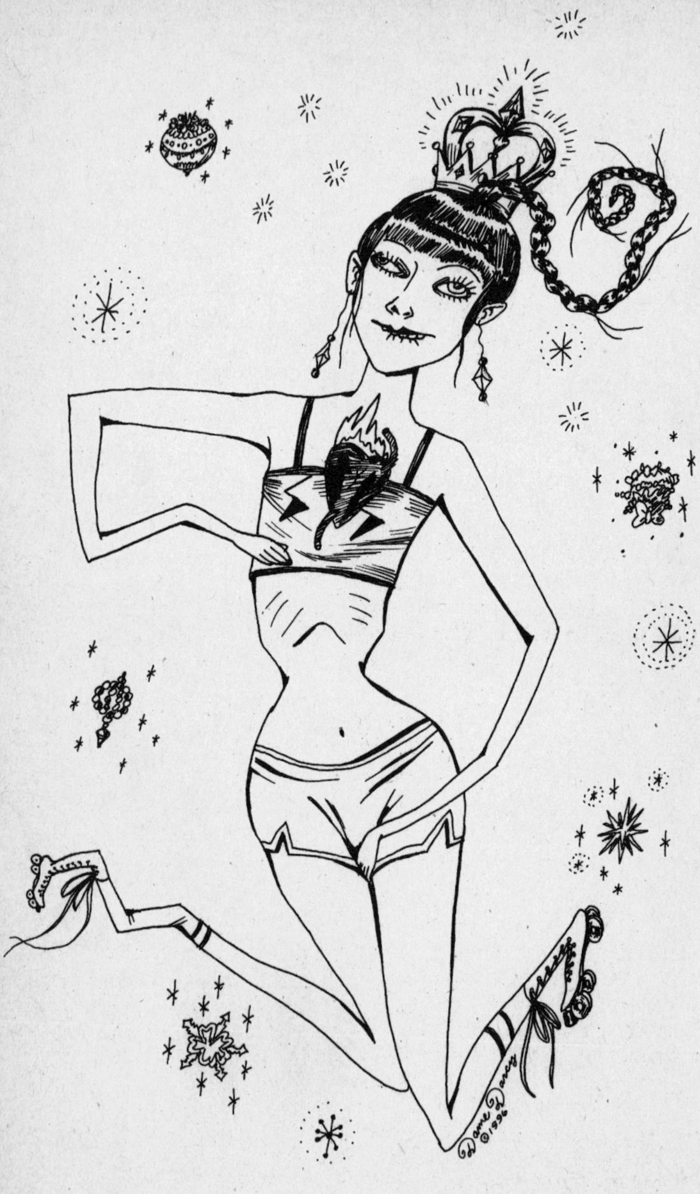
Dame Darcy
©1996

Dancing Queen

The Lusty
Adventures of
Lisa Crystal Carver

Lisa Carver

An Owl Book
Henry Holt and Company
New York

Henry Holt and Company, Inc.
Publishers since 1866
115 West 18th Street
New York, New York 10011

Henry Holt ® is a registered
trademark of Henry Holt and Company, Inc.

Published in Canada by Fitzhenry & Whiteside Ltd.,
195 Allstate Parkway, Markham, Ontario L3R 4T8.

Library of Congress Cataloging-in-Publication Data
Carver, Lisa.
Dancing queen: the lusty adventures of Lisa Crystal Carver/ Lisa Carver.
p.   cm.
"An Owl book."
1. Carver, Lisa.   2. Dover (N.H.)—Biography.   3. United States—
Social life and customs—1971–   4. Popular culture—United States.
I. Title.

CT275.C3415A3   1996   96-20834
814'.54—dc20   CIP

ISBN 0-8050-4392-6

Henry Holt books are available for special promotions and premiums.
For details contact: Director, Special Markets.

First Edition—1996

Designed by Brian Mulligan

Printed in the United States of America
All first editions are printed on acid-free paper.∞

1   3   5   7   9   10   8   6   4   2

This book is dedicated to my mother for making me so nice and normal, to my father for making me so weird and bad, and to my stepmother—a mean lady who scared me. But now that I'm all grown up, I am irresistibly drawn to mean ladies who scare me and I keep writing essays about them. (Don't get me wrong—my stepmother is fun and I like her.) And to my editor, Bryan Oettel, who never made me feel bossed around: he's a good man. Wish I could say the same for the rascals in this book.

CONTENTS

INTRODUCTION
The American

I always figured I'd write a book, but I thought it would be just like *Anna Karenina*—a big, huge book encompassing generations, the different races, country versus city, war, business, love and betrayal and childbirth and scenery—and I wouldn't write it till I was fifty. Then one day I realized I'm not Russian, and I'm not going to suddenly turn Russian when I'm fifty. I'm never going to have a ten-month winter to make me gloomy and deep and a good chess player, and I'm never going to have a long gray beard. I'm American. Always have been and I always will be. I'm zesty and smart and cute and sleazy and direct and confrontational. I'll never be elegant and I'll never have a long attention span. I eat Cheerios for breakfast and hot fudge sundaes for dessert. I yell at my TV. I'm enthusiastic, abrupt, self-obsessed, and I love boobs.

I grew up in Dover, New Hampshire. The most exciting thing ever to happen there didn't even happen: it was what a Dover history book calls "a contention" in 1623 between Capt. Thomas Wiggin, governor of one part of Dover, and Capt. Walter Neal, boss of another part. The two never did fight, but Capt. Wiggin did *carry* a sword around for a few days, so in light of what *might* have occurred, the place of the contention was named "Bloody Point."

New Hampshire's big claim to fame in modern times is that it's the number-one manufacturer of blankets in the nation.

There wasn't all that much for a budding wild woman to do in Dover in the late seventies and early eighties. There was one amusement park, but it was too far to get to. What you could do was swing on the park swings, make up dirty lyrics to the Oscar Mayer weiner theme song, and smoke cigarettes when one of your buddies stole a few from her parents. You waited in line to see *Saturday Night Fever* five times and *Grease* six times, and tried quite unsuccessfully to find love with the sweaty-handed boy sitting next to you.

My mother and I lived in a two-room apartment, and one Christmas she gave me a cardboard house from Sears—five feet by five by five. We put it up in a corner of our bedroom. Most of my lusty adventures in Dover, New Hampshire, happened right there in that cardboard house, in my daydreams. I'd crawl in and open my box of secret stuff, where drawings (mostly of naked people with huge organs and nipples pointing to the sky, doing things to each other) and charts and lists detailed my secret plots. I imagined how I would have an island where loaves of Wonder bread grew on bushes and I could decide who would live and who would die and what jobs everyone would have (ranging from island sweeper, who was my friend Ginger's annoying mom, to dictator, who was me). Or how I was going to run away as soon as I turned thirteen and be a prostitute and take drugs. Or how I was going to be just like Olivia Newton-John when I grew up: the prettiest woman in the whole world and a really good roller skater.

If it wasn't a school night and I was really lucky, my mother would drive me and all my friends, everyone sitting on everyone's lap in the Honda Civic, to Happy Wheels, the roller rink at the outskirts of town. The lights were so beautiful in a roller rink—strobe lights and red, blue, and yellow spotlights roaming the walls. When "Dancing Queen" by Abba would come on, I'd feel like a real queen dancing. One glittering skate held high behind me on a straight and regal leg, I was gliding through space and time and flashing lights. It was a true wonderland. Sadly, even with all the strobe lights making me extra good-looking, I found no love at the rink. My friend Ginger had a romance with one young Casanova on wheels, but we learned he'd been lying about being eleven—he was really only ten! That ended *that*.

The American is wild and free, and her country is big, so she must roam. When I was seventeen I left Dover for California with my best friend Rachel, who was sixteen and dropped out of school to come with me. Our stupidity amazes me. We just showed up at Los Angeles International Airport with one suitcase each. We thought that everyone was going to welcome us with open arms, saying, "We're going to make you stars! You sure have potential, ladies—we can see your glow." (We didn't definitely plan to be movie stars. We didn't definitely plan anything, except to be free and wonderful and magnificent, whatever that meant.) At the baggage claim the awful realization suddenly hit us: we knew absolutely no one, we had nowhere to go, and we didn't know what we were doing. So we sat down and cried. A kind policeman directed us to a youth hostel that had a ride board. Because Rachel didn't like the trees in Southern California—it seems they were too squat—we wrote down that we wanted to go north. An Australian named Ian gave us a ride. He was very bizarre. After a few hours he took out a knife and Rachel and I screamed, thinking he was going to murder us. Instead he cut some cheese for a snack. By then we were too spooked to go on, so we got out right there, in Hayward, California.

Hayward boasted fifty used car lots, a cemetery, and one horrible tenement, which we moved into right away. We had to bribe the landlord with three months' rent in advance, because he thought we were runaways. The landlord was named Don, but we secretly dubbed him "Long Dong." He got his name because his hot-stuff girlfriend was about four feet tall and four feet wide, and most of her body was breast, so we reasoned Don must have a long dong in order to accomplish "the act." That was the kind of stuff we used our reasoning powers on, which is why we had ended up in L.A. with no friends and no money.

We were after experience—any experience. We wanted wild love. We wanted our $25 fake I.D.s to get us into clubs (they didn't).

We considered ourselves diners at the feast of life—and our stomachs were rumbling!

We couldn't find jobs, and once our savings ran out our stomachs *really* started rumbling. Rachel returned to New Hampshire. I stayed on and found what might have been wild love when a sort of dumb jewelry seller in Berkeley held me up in the air for upside-down 69 while on acid. That was interesting, but a few days later he sniffled and said, with unfathomable self-pity, "I didn't mean to fall in love with you. I didn't think this would happen." I was gravely offended that someone would not *mean* to fall in love with me, and promptly broke up with him. At that age I was not after an empathetic or considerate life. My life would be grandiose, and the next step was to get a job at Honeybear Treat Yogurt.

After one month at Honeybear Treat I was accused of eating more than my allotted one yogurt cone per day and was fired. Lessie, the owner's slightly Latvian thirty-five-year-old henchwoman, had told on me. If the truth be known, I *was* eating more than my one cone per day—much more. I couldn't help it, I was hungry! It was good! I should've known from the start Lessie would tell. She had the look of a tattler, that smug set of lips, those big dark eyes that never blink. That damn Lessie told on me just two hours after I went to her house and bought a bicycle from her. Yeah, she got what she wanted out of me, all right. My $35. It took me nine hours to make that $35. And then the chain fell off on the way home! As you can see, I still have bitter feelings toward Lessie.

I knew there wasn't room enough in the state of California for both Lessie and me. Besides, the only jobs left in Hayward were selling used cars or cemetery plots, and I didn't think I had the right look for either one. So I decided to go back to New Hampshire too. The American is wild and free, but when she spends her last $35 on a stupid bike that breaks, she must run home.

Back in Dover, Rachel and I got jobs cleaning a factory at night.

After three weeks, I was fired for not vacuuming well enough (this was after two warnings), and Rachel immediately quit out of sympathy. We walked home in the freezing dark, two unemployed ladies in piles of negligee-like dresses rather than a heavy sweater like normal people would wear, expressing our shock that one could be so smart in some ways and so dumb in others. I mean, I really *tried* to vacuum well, and I just couldn't do it! But I didn't mind that much, 'cause I knew things other people didn't know.

All my life, I had seen secrets everywhere. I listened to the same songs, watched the same movies, shopped at the same K-mart as everyone else, but other people didn't seem to be receiving the incredible messages I heard between the lines, the barely disguised call to perversion I saw right there in the open, hidden on the surface.

I've done lots of stupid things, but I've enjoyed myself. *Dancing Queen* is about *liking* stuff. It's about how pleasing it can be to be poked and probed—by the hairdresser, by the gynecologist, by killer bears, by the thirty-year-old ski instructress in *Princess Daisy*. Lately I keep reading American magazine articles and books all about not liking things—a whole essay by a woman who was upset that some men hooted at her, for instance. I *like* to be hooted! I figure that's just their dumb manly way of paying a compliment. I mean, in the grand scheme of life, what's wrong with a hoot? Nothing! People are so sensitive these days! They think they're French or something. Americans have forgotten what's great about being American. It's not our sensitivity. It's our impatience, our changeability, our excitement, our openness, our cheer, our sexuality, our very crassness. We seem ashamed of our talk shows for their emotional explosions, their leaps from topic to topic, their rowdiness, their excess—but *that's* what's so great about America! Let other countries be patient. Let other countries be refined. Let other countries think all the time. They do it better anyway. I'd rather have a peanut butter sundae and do a little dance.

Poverty, all the sleazy pleasures and nowhere-left-to-fall free-doms it brings, is half of what made me what I am. The other half of me comes from scrambling to get out. One of Pa's speeches on *Little House on the Prairie* gave me hope as a young girl. Laura worked in a stable, and rich Nellie Oleson came by and called her a stinky stable girl. Pa told Laura, "Nellie can buy anything she wants and you can't. That's why the Lord gave you gifts with which you can get anything you need in life: he gave you determination, imag-ination, and a strong body." I thought, "Yeah—me, too! I'm a stinky welfare kid now, but I have determination and imagination and a strong body, and if I work hard enough, I can get everything I want." Of course, everything I wanted might've been a bit seedier than what Pa had in mind for Laura.

What being American meant in the pioneer days, and what it still means today for those with a little bravery, is to create one's own world. If you can't vacuum so great, just write a book about all the things you were dreaming of that were distracting you from notic-ing those specks in the corner. And everything will be wonderful in the end.

Dancing Queen

White Trash—

You Can Run

'Em Over With

Your Car and

They'll Still

Come After

You Hollering

I told everyone they better not get me no
sweater for Christmas. Not the shit they got
this year. Goddamn four, five colors in them.
I ain't no faggot.

—*a guy at Friendly's*

White Trash are very entertaining but very
horrible and very amazing. They're so strange
and violent. They do things I don't
understand. I like to watch them from my
window, but if I'm down there with them I get
very nervous and want to run away.

—*Dame Darcy*

No matter what time of day or night it was,
they'd be working on their car. How much
work can a car take? He had this girlfriend,
she was really sickly looking, and she'd work
on it with him. They'd talk in car-talk. It gave
'em something to do at four in the morning
when they were on crank.

—*Kerry McLaughlin*

$\mathcal{I}$t's not that I dislike the middle class. It's just that I like so much the inventiveness that poverty necessitates. Well, OK—I do dislike the middle class. How to do things is all laid out for you when you have enough money. You take vacations at vacation places, where you're told what to do for each minute of the day. When you're poor, your vacation is, say, camping out by the train tracks with your friends and dressing up a mannequin someone somehow acquired, leaving it on the tracks, and hiding where you can see what happens when the next train comes. You're resourceful!

Then the upper classes come along and pluck out the most beautiful and the smartest from the ranks of the poor, leaving the ugly, the loud, the lewd and the ignorant. Yep, those are my neighbors. That's my heritage . . . White Trash.

A White Trash heritage steers a person's behavior in a certain direction. It will cause her to laugh really loud at dumb stuff all the time, and then laugh even harder because she hears her own dumb laugh. She'll suddenly yell at some person across the room because she just got mad for no reason except that's just the way she is. Then she lights up a cigarette because it tastes good. She'll have sex with somebody (maybe the person she just yelled at). Then immediately afterwards she'll call up her friend to talk about it—and if he doesn't like it that she's doing this right in front of him, she'll just laugh more—'cause she's always pretty happy except for when she's mad (which is often).

New Hampshire, my home state, boasts a particularly boisterous breed of White Trash, especially the women. In New Hampshire if a woman's husband is treating her in a manner she doesn't care for, she'll hit him over the head with a broomstick and that's the end of it. In California, the White Trash women'll get together and drink wine and ponder on the problem. They tell each other they're gonna take back their maiden names and go get a hairdressing license, but you know it'll never happen. They should just grab a broomstick— it's cheaper.

▎take my friend Ethan, who comes from Kentucky, to visit my friend Debbie Flynn, who has lived in New Hampshire all her life. Debbie opens the door to us, lifts up her shirt, and scratches her protuberant belly, announcing, "I have PMS like a motherfucker." *General Hospital* is on TV, the phone is ringing, and Debbie's hair is yellow. "Debbie, Ethan. Ethan, Debbie," I say. Debbie picks up the phone and carries on conversations simultaneously with the caller and Ethan and me. Assuming Ethan is my new beau, Debbie tells him about my old boyfriends, asks about our sex life, and lets us know all about hers. The conversation with the caller is about a mutual friend (female) passing out topless on a sidewalk and then just getting up a few hours later and attending a barbecue. I love those tales of fortitude.

We go for a drive. Ethan stops at a yellow light. "Whatsamattuh, yain't got no f'ck'n' BALLS?" Debbie's supposed to be in the backseat, but she's leaning forward so far her head and shoulders are parallel to Ethan's and mine. Her mauve nails are digging into the vinyl seat, and spit's coming out of her mouth. Debbie is furious. Debbie doesn't like having her 90 mph body stuck in a zero mph car. "Wheredja get yeh license from—a Cracker Jacks box? Get yeh ass out there! Look at that guy there—he's got BALLS!" She's not yelling; she's barking. Seriously—she does not sound human.

"What did you think of Debbie Flynn?" I ask Ethan as soon as we leave.

"Man, I can't even believe that woman has a last name. I've seen a lot of White Trash in Kentucky, but *her*. . . ."

You can always spot White Trash—even if they miraculously go on to acquire a Ph.D. and move to Europe—by the unrefinable pasty complexion caused by a youth of nonstop Wonder bread and Chef Boyardee. Another surefire sign is alcoholism.

The New Hampshirite alcoholic White Trash's constitution is amazingly sturdy. The ones in New York always look on the point of death, and you always hear about them dying. New Hampshirite alcoholics, on the other hand, are robust with a frightening zest for life. We never die; we just have more babies.

Young New York or Jersey White Trash these days are a more arrogant breed than their New Hampshire contemporaries. Those cityfolk White Trash learn all this complicated kickboxing and a stock of verbal comebacks. Here in New Hampshire, fancy karate moves would probably make us pull a tendon—we just pound on each other. And for our repartee, "Fuck you, asshole!" never gets old. An example of New Hampshire White Trash humor is a grown man saying to an eight-year-old kid, "Look at this doll—do you want me to give it to you?" And when she says yes, he socks her with it and says, "There, I gave it to you!" and laughs uproariously. He then goes on "telling" the joke to every new young person he meets for the next ninety years until he finally dies at the age of a hundred and ten, as mean and dumb as he was at twenty—and just as jolly.

Acne, dried-out hair, and t-shirts advertising cigarette brands are a favorite look for White Trash females of all ages. Obesity is also in vogue. The ones that aren't fat are really thin, with weird, hard faces like diamonds—prominent eyes, chins sticking out, cheekbones that surely cut those brave enough to kiss the woman. Their chests are concave, but oddly enough there's still flab hanging from their upper arms.

When they have to talk, they have to talk—especially if they get to block the grocery store aisle for twenty minutes while doing so. White Trash women have a lot of trouble to discuss—disgusting minor medical problems and battles with the electric company, landlords and their menfolk. Or they'll talk tough about an absent female acquaintance who is a "bitch like no tomorrow!" Sometimes they get into dirty fistfights. While the men tend to hurl each other across the room or down the stairs, the women lean toward closer contact—scratching and biting and twisting each other's boobies. Sometimes if they're *really* mad at their husband they'll try to run him over with the truck. I once saw a man throw an enormous picnic table on another man. It was so big and heavy . . . how did he do it? Even more amazing, how did the other man just get up from under the table unhurt? And then they both laughed!

The guys wear baseball caps and no shirts. About one-third of them are fat. They're in and out of jail. The skinny ones tend to be in jail more often. They have wary, darting, haven't-slept-in-days eyes. But for such obvious drug abusers, they're quite healthy and happy in their own way. They holler outgoing greetings to each other like, "What are you doing, old turd?" And the "old turd" answers: "Going to hock my saw. Fifteen dollars they give you for a damn screw saw downtown. Shit—that ass! Hate him!" White Trash men aren't too picky when it comes to women. They always whistle at me even when I'm wearing sweatpants and carrying laundry. Come to think of it, that's when they like me best.

Both the men and women like to have sex. I know because of my neighbors. If there's one thing White Trash aren't, it's shy about expressing their pleasure. The act is usually over in two and a half minutes, but what a crazy two and a half minutes it is!

White Trash live on welfare checks, low-scale drug dealing, and blue collar jobs.

White Trash don't go to bed until the wee hours. Then their dirty little kids wake them up around 6 A.M., and they all spill out onto the front porch and driveway and the dead little lawn, and the mother tells the kids to "shut the fuck up, you fucking assholes." If one of the kids complains that his brother hit him, she says, "Well hit him back then!" The father jokes with the mother and the neighbors (who are always over) about blowjobs and stuff like that. Emptied beer cans fill the back of the pick-up truck that the guys are always leaning over to fix so you can see their butt crack. There are a few pick-ups, a gutted car or two—with the parts strewn across the lawn—and a motorcycle that these guys fiddle with, but nothing ever gets fixed or changed. Van Halen blares.

At first I didn't understand about class. Around seventh grade it became apparent to me that there were two major divisions of females in the school. The "Barbies" got cute boyfriends, were cheerleaders, did their homework, and went to work at the mall once they turned sixteen. They grew up to be bank tellers with husbands and children who didn't smell like stale sweat and alcohol and who didn't have to go to the hospital for stitches every other month after another brawl. The other class were the beasts who ruled the bathrooms with the triple threat of smoke, hairspray and mean words. These girls had the audacity to bleach their hair at the tender age of thirteen, ate the green M&Ms first "'cause they make you horny," worked at the greenhouse with a permit at the age of fourteen, and gave their paycheck to their mother because—even though they like to hawk louies, cuss, litter and get in fights—they're really quite kind. I recently read a book about the Siamese Fighting Fish: "a pugnacious fish with gaudy fins, a confirmed carnivore who will readily respond to an opportunity to fight." The author delicately suggested that Fighting Fish like to have sex a lot, too. That book could've been written about the green-M&M–eating class of Dover Junior High—those who grew up to be White Trash.

I didn't exactly fit in with either group: the green-M&M–eaters

hollered threats that they were going to beat me up; the Barbies didn't holler threats at me—because they didn't say *anything* to me. So I felt closer to the green-M&M element. And I'm glad, because I don't think I would've made a good bank teller.

I like White Trash quite a bit. Sure they're obnoxious, uneducated, a bit rough with their kids, gross, and loud at night when you're trying to sleep, but they could teach my upset, vacillating, guilt-ridden Generation X peers a thing or two about pure joy and enthusiasm. White Trash are never, ever deterred by angst, scruples or a bad snowstorm from doing whatever they want with whomever they want, whenever and wherever. Sure, they could be more considerate of the environment, they could try not to use Styrofoam plates or be so loud at their cookouts or throw cigarette butts on the sidewalk. Sure, most of 'em actually believe the *National Enquirer*, but I've always found gullible people more pleasant than cynical ones. And yes, they often show poor judgment—but at least they don't have what my moralistic peers do have: so very much *good* judgment it keeps them from having any life at all. Sometimes the middle class do have sex and argue and stuff, but they generally (there are exceptions!) don't do so with the same gusto and unguilt as their trashy counterparts. Sometimes I just feel so *wild* using a Styrofoam plate, knowing it's not going to disintegrate for a thousand years!

The reason for a White Trash person's unguilt could be that she or he has never heard of Freud. Even if she or he does later chance upon mention of the man (probably in the context of a dirty joke), it's too late—the guilt rolls off the trash-coated heart like rain off a WD-40'ed distributor cap.

Recently I was asked to submit an essay for a book on White Trash, and the editor sent me a description of the book. He seemed like a nice man, and I certainly don't wish to insult him, but everything he said could not have been more wrong. He decried the "pejorative naming practice" of calling White Trash "White Trash," pleading instead for "state assistance, respectful treatment and good working conditions" for these "disempowered" people.

I thought: "What? You think you have more power sitting there *writing* than a guy who has twelve *engines* in his backyard? Say there's a nuclear war or some other catastrophe, what would be more important to a survivor: a fancy vocabulary or the ability (that just about all White Trash have) to fix a leaking roof or get a car going or shoot a shotgun?

"As for your respect: White Trash doesn't deserve it. They're brawling drunks who yell at their kids and leave a mess wherever they go. Furthermore, they don't *want* your respect. They don't *like* people who use words like *disempowered.* Sure they'd like to win the lottery, but they don't spend their time feeling bad about not being empowered with money—they have more urgent matters to think about, like finding Ronnie who slept with Bob's woman so they can beat him up. *That's* the kind of stuff White Trash worry about.

"And good working conditions? They're strong. Nothing can kill them—not mines, not precarious roofing jobs, not pumping gas in the freezing cold on Christmas Day. Let there be *someone* left on earth strong enough to take lousy working conditions, sixteen-hour shifts, and getting all stinky and filthy. Corporate housewives have to have *some* dirty laborers left to fantasize about."

It's starting to be hip to be White Trash. All these people are going around claiming to be Trash; they don't want to be thought of as wimpy middle class. But these people are far from qualified— they're too educated, too existential, too sensitive, not spontaneous enough, not brutally honest enough. First of all, White Trash would never claim to be White Trash—they don't know they are. They just think they're "real people," as opposed to being "fruits" or "foreigners" or "people who think too much."

This new, hip White Trash do some of the same things as the real

White Trash, but they just have altogether too many *reasons* for doing it. They watch *Roseanne* "because it's so White Trash." True Trash watch *Roseanne* because it's on. Hip Trash shop in thrift shops for tacky, out-of-fashion clothes. True Trash think shopping at thrift stores is beneath them; they go to K-mart. True White Trash don't *try* to be tacky; they *are*.

In my darkest hours I wonder—what if I'm one of the "hip" White Trash and don't know it? Oh, how terrible! The other day I caught myself using the word *circumscribe* casually in conversation. I was horrified—was I now automatically disqualified from the lower classes? But then I got to thinking about how *circumscribe* sounds like *circumcise*, which made me start laughing (anything related to sexual organs—no matter how casually—still makes me laugh), so I guess I'm still in the running. Surely there's a drop of middle-class blood in my veins, for even though I was a welfare kid who wore feather earclips, shit-kickers (Timberline boots) and smoked a pack a day at age eleven (quit at age twelve), my mother wouldn't let me use double negatives, and I appreciate experimental films now and stuff like that . . . still, nothing cracks me up like a good burp. Not only that, but one time my ex-mother-in-law was chasing me around the luggage turnstile at the airport with her hand raised, screaming, "You piece of shit! I'm going to slap you to pieces." There's only one class of people that get chased around luggage turnstiles by enraged sixty-five-year-old women in puffy cat decal sweatsuits—the fun class.

Desperate and Twelve—Princess Daisy, Quasimodo, Heathcliff, Cliff Craddock, Marquis de Sade and Me

SHE WAS AN INNOCENT LASS . . . One
moment lovely Prudence Walker was living
the life of a dutiful orphan; the next she was
lying in a highwayman's arms. Wounded in a
foiled robbery attempt and thoroughly
drenched from a storm, the dreaded Scot
bandit seemed harmless enough. Or so
Prudence thought—until the infamous rogue
stole her breath and her will with his honeyed
kisses, until she felt the rapier-sharp edge of
his sensuous charm.

—back cover of
Heather and Velvet
by Teresa Medeiros

𝓟ut a dark, brutal but noble and all-knowing stranger in the grubby hands of a dreamy eleven- or twelve-year-old girl and what've you got? A romance novel. Eleven- and twelve-year-old girls like to imagine being treated with impropriety, talking back to the rude stranger in a fiery way, fleeing, and then being caught and totally loved. Reading and thinking about that stuff is what inspires girls to learn masturbation. We're emotional and imaginative creatures—we don't want to look at the blunt instruments paraded openly in *Playgirl*. We want to dream of awful and wonderful things befalling us on the moors, or being roughed up by some foreign hijackers and then having one fall in love with us. Fantasies of incest go over big with girls, too. (Perhaps I should make it clear that I am not proposing you male readers go commit incest, nor that you hijack a plane and feel up a passenger.)

At twelve, I had as much sex drive as the entire U.S. Army and absolutely no idea what to do with it. I hadn't even learned how to masturbate yet—well, I hadn't learned how to masturbate *well*. I was skinny and socially incompetent . . . and *on fire*. No matter what I did to try to get lucky, it didn't work. I got a perm and wore blue eyeshadow and red lipstick and hung out at Funspot, Dover's video arcade/preteen pickup joint, and all that happened was I became the champ at Frogger. I stuffed my bra, and two boys accused me of stuffing. (I had gone home from school Friday flat-chested and I thought no one would be surprised if I showed up on Monday with C cups.) I even put a sunflower seed in my naked vagina hoping to tempt my gerbil Newton to forage for it. Though Newton was the greatest stud in the gerbil kingdom, even he was uninterested in me.

I was romantic and dreamy, burdened with too much love to give, and no one wanted even a little portion of it. Well, there was Steve McKenny, at Brandon Kelly's party who, when we were both drunk on Brandon's parents' vodka, motioned me into a tent and humped my leg like a poodle until I ran away. I suppose I could've let him hump my leg and then I could have humped his, but I was so filled with fantastic love images that accepting mutual leg-humping would've been like taking a job at a gas station when you're sure you're just *this* far away from being made queen of all the world.

And so sex eluded my hips and bloomed wildly in my mind. My fantasies were outrageously cruel and inventive, often physically impossible. I wanted to be molested by ten men, I wanted to hang some of my female classmates from the Junior High hallway ceiling and impale their special spot with a vibrator made in the shape of a hammer. A classmate with an older brother lent me a Marquis de Sade book, and I thought the chapter in which the girl is kidnapped and has horrible sex things done to her was *very* good. I didn't truly wish for anyone to be hurt (including myself)—I was just excessively enthusiastic. If only I could've *done* it, I would've known sex for the delightful but not all-consuming thing that it is. As it was, I was quite consumed. I saw sex everywhere and in everything. Pop-Tarts going into the toaster slots looked pretty lascivious to me. I pictured everyone, no matter how old or unlikely, doing it.

Besides that Marquis de Sade book, I read approximately a Harlequin per day throughout seventh grade. I read them while I ate, while I walked, while I bathed . . . I lived in a dream. The Harlequin heroine never gets much character development, so the reader can easily insert herself in the role. So at least once a day throughout junior high, a flinty-eyed, rich thirty-five-year-old man took my glasses off and recognized my true beauty. Completely overwhelmed, he had to marry me at once.

Once I had read all fifty thousand Harlequins, I moved on to more lurid romantic novels that taught me everything I needed to know about dark secrets, good-looking kidnappers and sowing seeds into people.

HARLEQUIN PRESENTS . . .

This series, with books featuring subtitles such as "Secrets: Everyone Has Something to Hide" or "Too Hot to Handle," followed the Harlequin formula exactly, except they used certain words assiduously avoided in Harlequins: words like *panties*.

Eighteen-year-old Amanda has no idea what effect she has on men. That is, until Cliff Craddock comes along, and the heat of his steady, flinty stare makes her quite aware of what makes her different from the boys. His eyes are like chips of stone. He's had some bad experiences with women—they try to capture him because he's so rich and mesmerizingly good-looking and unattainable. He has his fun with them, but is aware of their conniving, and in the end they mean nothing to him. Amanda, not yet trained by Cliff in the virtues of yielding, is headstrong. Thrown together by an unlikely series of events, she and Cliff have lots of tiffs. During a particularly heated row, Cliff cups Amanda's firm, young breasts. Against her will, her body shudders. Her heart is racing. She must not surrender to the intense feelings exploding inside her. She must think of Charles, the beau her aunt wants for her—gentle, reliable Charles. But, she forgets. She melts in Cliff's embrace, ready to give him everything. Her untutored but nevertheless hot kisses tell him she's a virgin. Abruptly, he stops what he's doing. He has decided to make Amanda his wife. But he doesn't tell her (for he is a man of few words). *Why did he stop?* Amanda wonders. *Am I not as skilled as the countess?* (The countess is one of those conniving women roaming Cliff's castle.) Amanda is unaware that her lack of "skills" has skillfully captured the uncapturable heart of Cliff Craddock. Feeling shame and confusion, she flees—flees Cliff, his castle, his beautiful gray eyes, and is about to flee the whole country when he finds her and does everything but *that* to her. Poor Amanda gets confused and angry *again!* (For reasons the reader is not told, but which must be good ones, Cliff still hasn't revealed his penetration-abstaining motives to Amanda.) She runs away a second time and befriends a small child. Unbeknownst to Amanda, Cliff is watching her. He realizes Amanda is good with children. The sun is setting. Cliff's hard eyes turn soft with love as he comes out from behind that bush and takes her in his arms—gently, yet in a hard way, too. "Tomorrow we will marry," he says huskily, "and then I will show you all I've held off from so far." "Oh," Amanda sighs, "I can hardly wait till then." Cliff, smothering her with hot kisses, says, "I've waited a *lifetime* for you, my darling."

My cheeks are burning.

VICTORIA HOLT,
Queen of the Gothic Romance

Victoria Holt is so extreme—all her stories include death by poison, treachery, a mentally retarded servant or two and some dark secret. She has written about a million novels, and they're all good. In one, the man, who I recall was the Compt Somebody-or-Other, practically rapes a woman and she falls in love with him! She moves in with him . . . him and his mistress! Eventually the Compt realizes he's in love with her, they get married, and the mistress goes away.

The Victoria Holt heroine is always running away and the man follows her. My God, I like the guys that can't be stopped. You know he's really forceful and he's not gonna end up sitting on his butt all day watching TV. Just think—some brutal man absconding with you! He'd be brutal, but kind to you. He might even be a murderer (though he'd never murder you, of course). You flee to another country and he follows you because you're everything to him. And he of course knows where to find you. He knows how to do everything. I wish a man like that would come into my life . . . but if he did, he'd probably rape me, and I'd be so scared and run to the police. But in the stories the heroine is irresistibly drawn. He's really honorable deep down inside, but he's just so *forceful* he can't *help it.* The thing is, it's 1700 and things were different then. (Lately I reread two Victoria Holt novels, and they seemed quite tame and completely unlike what I just described. Perhaps it's like repressed memory syndrome—that new fad where you remember twenty years later that you were molested when most likely you weren't.)

ON THE JUDITH KRANTZ ROADMAP OF LOVE, ALL HIGHWAYS LEAD TO TROUBLEVILLE

At some point in every person's pre-adolescence, there is one book or movie that unhooks the latch that was just barely holding back a flood of perversity. Lifelong fantasies are just forming, and the particular book becomes a roadmap to the young reader's entire sexual future. My friend "Itchie" read *Clan of the Cave Bear* by Jean Auel over and over, about a girl who gets transported back to Cro-Magnon times. In it, every time a certain ugly fellow in the clan does a certain hand gesture to our heroine, she must drop whatever it is she's doing and get on her hands and knees and guess what happens then. This caused Itchie to always go out with Cro-Magnon types, even though she always ends up not liking them. My friend Rachel's floodgates were opened by a more civilized book, *Scruples* by Judith Krantz. The plot was a bunch of rich people go shopping. Rachel was hoping to live like the main character—cold, rich, with a husband who would support her but not touch her. She planned to be haughty and dress in couture. Rachel got all worked up over the thought of being cold and haughty.

The delicious Judith Krantz formula is that something horrible happens to you—like your brother or your female neighbor seduces you against your will—thus you don't have to admit to wanting sex but you get to have it anyway. Then they fall in love with you but you can still be haughty 'cause you can hold something over them (they raped you). Feeling guilty, they support you, and you become fabulously wealthy.

"I thought it would all be like that, too, once I got out of Dover," Rachel once confessed to me. "Leave my humble beginnings behind. Then my real life would begin—my Judith Krantz life—and I'd wear hats all the time . . . hats with veils."

The book responsible for unleashing the dirty floodwater of my imagination was a Judith Krantz book, too—*Princess Daisy*. I was in bed at a neighbor's house at the time of introduction, sick, sick, sick with the flu. I was delirious. During a lull in my fever, the neighbor, surely not realizing the demoralizing effect it would have on me, put the red-hot book in my hot little hands. Why, if that hadn't happened, who knows how I would have turned out!

Three scenes added to my fever that day—the memory of which can to this day make me shiver and roll my eyes:

1. The brother Ram seducing his sister Daisy. She barricades her door against him every night but one, and that night he creeps in. Gently he touches the sleeping Daisy with swirling motions until her hips start stirring in her sleep. But that gets him too excited, he can't control himself and he has his way with her hard and quick.

2. The thirty-year-old ski instructress seducing the confused fifteen-year-old student, Stash. She makes him undress. She laps him all over, but won't let him move or touch her. When he is half-crazy with desire and frustration, she "lowers her parted lips down on the straining shaft with all the leisure of her thirty years." (I haven't opened the book in fifteen years, but you don't forget a line like that.) Afterwards, he is confused no more, and becomes arrogant, demanding cocoa and a hot bath, and then they do it again.

3. Oh, I can barely even tell this last one! A woman with long nails seduces the wife of her husband's friend. Topsy cannot believe she has become *so* excited just by having her nipples sucked and fingertips touched. I cannot say more. It's just too much. After they do it, Miss Long Nails asks Topsy if she will wear a garter belt and stockings when the two married couples go yachting together the next week. Topsy says, "Oh God . . . yes." Unfortunately, the hot, close atmosphere of this scene is dispersed by having one of the husbands named Ham.

WUTHERING HEIGHTS—
A Wandering Fiend

If any book should be banned, it's this one. Heathcliff was so awful—he hung that poor lady's poodle! It's unforgivable. I know that, and still my life has been stricken by the phantasm of the dark-eyed Heathcliff roaming the moors and digging up his true-love's grave. "Would he dig up my grave to embrace my rotting corpse, mad with love and grief?" I ask myself about every prospective boyfriend. The answer is generally no, and then I feel contemptuous of him and I'm mean to the poor fellow and he has no idea why. I know other young ladies do that, too. Many a man has suffered for not being Heathcliff.

V. C. ANDREWS—
You Can't Help It When You're Locked in
the Attic with Your Good-Looking Brother

We young readers all pictured ourselves imprisoned by our evil grandmother and a mother who would rather party than raise four kids, in that attic with the gay paper flowers and the two enormous paintings depicting hell, forced through isolation to commit incest with our beautiful blond brother who looks exactly like us . . . and we become pregnant and have to plan a dangerous escape!

FABIO—
A Modern Lover (He's always mentioning condoms in his pirate books)

Fabio left Italy without his father's blessings to come to America to be a Bodice-Ripper man-model. He did a good job. Not content to be merely the most popular romance book cover model *ever*, he then recorded a really long come-on over sexy music: *Fabio After Dark*. He also decided to write his own romance novel, but instead of writing it he decided to "emote" into a tape recorder, and a female transcriber worked the, let's say, *raw* material into book form. His books are called *Pirate* and *Rogue* and maybe *Rascal*. They contain bold lines like:

1. "I am a man of the sea."
2. "Go hide in the fields, woman."[1]
3. "Mayhaps she thinks I am doing something bad."[2]

What modern man is a man of the sea? Only Fabio.

THE HUNCHBACK OF NOTRE DAME

A favorite among the more intellectual set of young masturbators. The best scene is when the priest—who is sexy in a rigid, moralistic

[1] Well, the line is really "Go hide in the fields." I was just interpreting for Fabio when I added "woman." I like to think he meant *go hide in the fields and I'll come find you.*

[2] My friend Boyd Rice suggests the next line: "By and by I'll learn her different."

way—can't help himself from placing his dirty hand on the sleeping Esmirelda's pure white breast. Her screams summon Quasimodo, the reviled hunchback, who runs in and punches the priest, his mentor, and just *grabs* Esmirelda and *throws* her over his shoulder like a gunny sack and runs to the top of the church. He's so big and strong. Death, deformity and tragedy add a moving quality to this most cherished masturbation fantasy.

?

My mother's friend lent her a book that featured disturbingly enormous, raised flowers on the cover. I was only able to sneak a read of one scene: a man rips the woman's diaphragm out and *throws* it across the room and has his way with her. It was scary but exciting. I was only eleven and I thought a diaphragm was a part of a woman's body. He mentioned something about sowing his seed into her. I like books where the characters really have their way with somebody.

Beside romance novels, I read a lot of science fiction. While I never did imagine having love activity with space aliens, these books did contribute to better sex later in life by teaching me at a young age how to warp and expand my perceptions of time and space. This ability really comes in handy when, say, you and your loved one are visiting your parents and the only place you can do it is in the bathroom, and if you don't want to arouse suspicion you'd better be done in five minutes.

What romance novels taught me was the excruciating joys of tension and waiting, and that if he has gray eyes he's probably the one. They also showed me the horrifying fate awaiting those who follow the troubling instinct to do what you shouldn't with whom you shouldn't when you shouldn't . . . and how great it is while you're doing it.

Anyone who thinks a five-foot-tall kid with a runny nose and highwater pants is too young to be sexually charged is nuts. Virgins are more sex-obsessed than even those people who own sixteen vibrators and go to swap-a-mate weekend retreats. I wondered about naked people and what they did to each other *all the time* when I was twelve. So did my friends. Those romance books really fed the fire! Within those pages, no one just had sex in bed; there was all sorts of odd and intricate, extremely passionate, sometimes even illegal sexual activity going on. Throughout most of junior high, I actually had rugburn scabs on my knees and elbows from amorous activities with pillows. Since trading pillows in for people, I hardly ever get scabs. I have gotten into many a messy situation, though, and I blame it all on the romance novels. They fanned my imagination in all the bad ways! They sold me a roadmap to ecstasy covered in highways of trouble, and I couldn't wait to visit every site on the map.

Killer Bear

$\mathcal{S}$ome ladies go wild over wolves. They fawn over the animal's intelligence and loyalty, and secretly imagine themselves the mate of the alpha male, running at his side at the front of the pack. They write books with anthropomorphic titles like *Our Brother, The Wolf.* Other girls fantasize about horses. I can see the attractive qualities: the loss of the maidenhead while riding a large, muscular, foaming creature with big, soulful eyes . . . secret orgasm . . . the wind in your hair, a noble beast to take you there. But for me, no animal will do but the one the Indians called "The King of the Brutes." He's the largest carnivore. He has beady little eyes, long claws and a whole lot of fur. He can survive four bullets to the heart just long enough to do something terrible to you. He likes to crush skulls and disembowel children and suck the marrow from their bones. He's a bear.

Ursus horribilus can reach 15 feet, weigh up to 2,000 pounds and run 30 miles per hour.

When a person survives a bear mauling, it's usually because the hungry bear ate only part of his victim and then buried the rest under leaves and dirt, intending to save our hero or heroine for two or three days, when his or her meat will get good and tender and juicy. This brave half-a-human will then crawl to the highway and hitch a ride to the hospital, undergo a year of reconstructive surgery, and then sell his or her story to *Readers' Digest*, thrilling impressionable young readers like me.

Here is some popular wisdom about the bear: if you want to find out if it's a black bear or a grizzly, kick it in the rump then climb a tree. If it follows you, it's a black bear. If it stays at the base of the tree hollering, it's a grizzly. When a teacher told this story to his class, an old man—a hunter—stood up and said, "I got a quicker test. Kick it in the rump and if you're still alive two seconds later, it's a black bear. If you're dead, it's grizzly."

Bears have a big appetite. Around 1955 in New Hampshire a black bear killed twenty-seven cows. Sometimes bears kill moose and eat them. Sometimes bears eat each other. One hunter checked the stomach contents of a bear he'd killed. He found a fawn *and* a bear cub, "feet, teeth, skull, bones, skin, everything." You'd think after eating a whole fawn, one would wait to digest and pass it before moving on to eat a little baby of one's own kind!

Bear-against-bear fights yield broken jaws, shattered teeth, missing eyes and, often, death. The female bear, called a sow, won't have sex with Mr. Bear, called a boar, when she's raising her cubs—which usually takes two years! This could explain why the bear sometimes gets so irritable he has to go on a killing spree; it also explains what happens at the end of one of my favorite fantasies.

In my twelfth summer I found under the passenger seat of my father's truck a dirty magazine featuring a pictorial of a picnicking girl approached by a bear . . . and they made love! My favorite photo was when he takes a swipe at her breast with his fearsome paw and she looks scared. It was the first dirty magazine I'd ever seen and I couldn't wait till it was dark so I could lie in bed and think about it. At last the time came, I narrowed my eyes and the glow-in-the-dark stars on my ceiling turned into real stars, and my killer bear fantasy unfolded. . . .

My friends Jeannie and Marie, my uncle Milt and I had been hiking all day. Milt had been pushing us the whole time, never letting us rest. When I said my ankles were killing me, Uncle Milt laughed and said, "It's good for you!" Jeannie called him a slave driver, and Milt said, "That's right!" and roared with obscene laughter. Finally, when it was quite dark and we had reached a thickly wooded, completely isolated area, Uncle Milt decided to allow us to quit our trudging. We set up two tents—one for the girls, one for Milt. In our crowded tent, Jeannie was taunting Marie, who was religious, with tales of her sexual exploits. Jeannie was big and developed and sort of dumb-looking, Marie was small and had a big nose and squinty eyes.

"My mother says you're going to be pregnant by the time you're fourteen, Jeannie," I informed her.

"Your mother shouldn't run her mouth about people she doesn't know," retorted rude Jeannie. "And you can tell your big, fat mother that she can kiss my sweet cheeks!"

"She's not big and fat!"

"Her brain is!"

"That's it—I'm bookin'." Among twelve-year-olds, that meant leaving. I took my sleeping bag and left the tent, seethed for a while, and then fell asleep.

I awoke to what sounded like a rifle shot. It was a clap of thunder. Lightning lit the sky, followed quickly by another clap of thunder, but no rain yet. I lay naked atop my sleeping bag—must've crawled out of my clothes in my sleep. The night was hot and close. The beasts of the forest were excited by the storm; there was a great deal of squawking and scurrying and squeaking. Insects swarming, buzzing. Another burst of lightning revealed a big, furry brown bear sauntering on his hind legs toward Uncle Milt, who was pointing his rifle at him. A shot rang out. "I got him!" Uncle Milt yelled, and then the bear plucked the gun out of Uncle Milt's hands and squeezed it in two. Jeannie and Marie struggled out of their tent just in time to see the bear rip Milt's scalp off his head. It looked like when a breeze whips a balding man's "comb-over" off his bare dome. "Girls! Help me! Hit him!" cried Milt just before the bear clawed his right eye out. Then Uncle Milt's head disappeared into the bear's giant mouth, and he was being shaken like a sock in a dog's mouth. The bear dropped Milt's body. Uncle Milt was dead.

Jeannie and Marie were trying to escape up a tree, moving in slow-motion as in a nightmare. The bear scooped up both of them—one in each arm. He took his time readjusting the girls so that he held them by their legs with their heads facing the same way. Both girls were squirming. "God help me!" Marie sobbed. "Help me, Jesus!" A lightning bolt leapt out of the sky in response, but it did not strike the bear.

"I'm not ready to die! Please, please, noooo!" screamed the sensuous young Jeannie. But Mr. Bear showed no mercy. He didn't care that the two girls, one pious and one lusty, were young and so much of their lives was yet unlived. With a mighty roar, he swung them by their legs against the tree they had tried to climb, breaking their bodies in two. Then he carefully lowered the girls to the ground to examine his handiwork. Marie's and Jeannie's bodies were held together in one piece only by a few thick tendons and strips of flesh. Jeannie's rib cage was standing at attention. The grizzly's thick, hard nails tore into the conquered flesh. Miraculously, Marie was still alive. But her horrible moans ceased abruptly, replaced by wet animal snorts as a shaggy muzzle was buried in her bubbling blood. After only one minute of carnage, it was impossible to tell which body parts belonged to which of my two dead friends.

Throughout the attack, I remained where I was, naked atop my sleeping bag. I heard in sixth grade that bears ignore what they believe to be dead meat, so that's what I was pretending to be. But he could sense that I was having my period (another fantasy—my body caught up to my gung-ho mind only very slowly, and I didn't actually get it till age fourteen and a half), and so the bear drew close and reared. I felt strangely calm while examining the beast towering over defenseless me. Blood-flecked foam gurgled out of his nose and mouth—he must have been hurt bad by Uncle Milt's rifle shot. Jeannie's and Marie's and Milt's blood, too, glinted in the starlight on Mr. Bear's chest. He licked between my legs. Though terrified, I knew I must stay perfectly still and not make a sound. After what seemed like an eternity, the bear, excited, began having his way with me. His kisses filled my mouth with the sickening sweet smell and taste of blood—mine, his, and that of my friends and my uncle. It lasts forever.

Sun streams through the silent forest. I see the movement of a bright red bird, yet no cry does he make. I'm pinned from the chest down 'neath the bear, who will never move again. A river of blood has congealed between us—soon the flies will come. I yawn and stretch my arms; it's a glorious new day.

How I Learned to "Do It"— I Was a Teenage Stalker

*W*hat do kids in the city *do* exactly? They kill each other, I imagine, but how many hours a day does that take? There's this perception that there are all these cultural opportunities for city kids, but no one ever gives the details. I mean, how many times do you feel like visiting the museum of fine arts when you're thirteen? There's also the perception that small-town kids must be bored, but in Dover we never were. We had a lot to do, and it all involved pursuing the opposite sex. Sometimes literally (if they ran away). Well, the actual pursuing took only about ten minutes a week and was rarely successful, but the plotting out of the pursuits, and the intensive post-pursuit analysis, took about five *hundred* hours a week!

It all started in sixth grade. Ginger was twelve and chewed her nails. I was eleven. Ginger liked this guy named Robert, and I liked this guy named Joey. We would sleep over at each other's house every weekend and play a game. "What would you do if Robert did this?" "I would let him." "What would you do if Robert did *this*?" "I would . . . I think I would make him wait until the next date. Hey! Cut that out! Now your turn. What would you do if Joey did *this*?" Intricately coded messages passed back and forth in the coat room between friends of the parties involved revealed that Robert found Ginger to be "a good kid, but not as a girlfriend," and the closest I ever got to the real Joey was when I flopped down into the seat next to him at the movie theater, at which point he got up and moved to the other end of the row.

Ginger ditched me in seventh grade—she was placed in Gemini, coded by the school faculty for the second smartest kids; they were the most popular kids. I was placed in Capricorn, the smartest kids, who no one liked because they were such nerds. I didn't like them either. When we were high school seniors, Ginger was voted "Most Considerate." She then went to college, dropped out, worked at a drugstore, got fat, went bleach blond and plucked her eyebrows into two little lines. I liked the eyebrows. Robert went on to become "Bob," went to the hospital via ambulance in tenth grade for alcohol-related liver problems, and I stopped seeing much of him in the halls after that. Joey became "Joe" and a cokehead. He was voted "Nicest Eyes" in eighth grade and looked twenty-five in ninth grade. A few years ago, I happened to work with him at a fish shop for three days before I got fired. He didn't remember me.

More intelligent, fun and sophisticated than Ginger was my ninth-grade friend Cheryl. By sophisticated I mean capable of creating and sustaining intricate situations. Neither of us had ever had a boyfriend, and we really wanted one. We looked like two creeps— a year younger than our classmates, skinny, flat-chested and victims of acne and last year's fashions—but we were *on fire* with sexual energy. To make ourselves more attractive, we had "pig-out" sessions (ate whole tablesful of food), searched around for the most effective over-the-counter soldier against zits (Fostex) and read *Cosmopolitan* religiously. We knew all about how we would handle a one-night stand and we hadn't even had one night where a boy *stood* near us. We spent the entire school day making up a secret language and exchanging coded notes about our passion for Chin and Z-dog. "Chin" earned his code name because he had none. He was the one I was hot for. "Z-dog" was named after the van of hit-radio WERZ, to which we imagined this object of Cheryl's desire must listen. At one point we switched off—Z-dog became my secret ideal and Cheryl started chasing after Chin. When it came to famous people, Cheryl liked Rick Springfield and I liked Ivan Lendl.

But we weren't just sitting around, waiting for these men to discover our inner beauty. Both Cheryl and I worked at Dunkin'

Donuts, and we loved to fill the doughnuts, because when you turned the jelly machine on, the metal counter vibrated, and as luck would have it, the edge was at just the right level! We were always daring each other into new adventures. We played tic-tac-toe with grease paints on each other's bodies. We'd do anything on a dare: streak through the neighborhood at midnight dressed in only bald-head wigs and high heels, pee in the lilac bushes outside my house, make obscene phone calls, and stay up all night. We bought a skeleton key and broke into the Masonic Temple. (Boy, was *that* disappointing! They must take all the secret ritualistic stuff home at night.) We stalked innocent passersby (believing them to be criminals), leaping from rooftop to rooftop and throwing ice cubes at them (so the evidence would melt). We finally made it official by deciding we had a spy service: Mystic Calling. We had cards made up, but no one ever asked us to do any spying.

Cheryl went on to be voted "Nicest Hair," attend law school and get married to the most boring man in the world, named Ted. The wildest sexual game they shared was for him to make her nipple hard and then hang his key ring off it. I couldn't believe she could go from *me* to *him*. Chin and Z-dog both went on to become flaming homosexuals. I hear they kissed each other in a pool one night but didn't like it.

In tenth grade my lockermate Ellen and I decided to get picked up. We'd never done this before, but it was easy because Ellen was blond and stacked. It happened on a bench on Miracle Mile. Miracle Mile had McDonald's, Taco Bell and Service Merchandise, and that's where those over sixteen and hungry for love would cruise at 15 miles per hour, inspecting those too young to have a driver's license, seated on the benches. Two men came over to us. Ellen did all the talking. Next thing you know, we hopped into their car and drove out into the woods, where we drank three Haffenraffer beers each.

I don't know if my guy was actually good-looking, but he was a *college freshman*, so I figured he must be handsome. I let him put his hands between my legs (outside the panties), but I didn't feel anything. The Haffenraffers (which, like my date, were extra strong and dark) were making me numb. I fended off his advances to my breasts, horrified at the thought of a man—a college man—finding out how undeveloped I was. Guessing my thoughts, he said, "Don't worry if they're small." I was mortified. In the front seat, Ellen was in the process of administering a second blowjob to her guy. Everything started spinning and being hilarious, and I just managed to fall out the car door before peeing all over my nylons while Ellen tried for three. With the one college man having had too much love and the other realizing that, not only was he not going to get any, but that at this point he didn't even *want* it anymore, it was decided that the girls would be driven home now.

Ellen peed her pants in the hallway, then tripped over a lamp and broke it. (She was sleeping over my house.) My mother woke up and grounded me for three months, and threatened to call Ellen's parents in the morning, but she never did. Right after we graduated, Ellen gained about 150 pounds, and that's about all I know of her.

Eventually I stopped being confused and awkward and scared around the opposite sex and my after-hours adventures became fulfilling and adroit, but there's something wonderfully alive about confusion and bad sex and fear, and I don't regret one second of my lousy early sex life. Of course, I'm not upset that it improved, either.

An Iron Fist

in a Polyester

Glove:

Lawrence Welk

Lawrence tells everyone what to do with a big cheeseball smile and everybody does it, with the same cheeseball smile back.

> —*Dame Darcy*

Lawrence Welk is the man who creates his own world and convinces so many people to believe in it—and look at the world he's created. . . . It's so beautiful!

> —*Jaina Davis*

The show—all the colors—it's an exotic fishtank of beautiful songs and dances. It's reassuring.

> —*Matt Jasper*

$\mathcal{D}$**uring practice,** this trumpet player had to go to the bathroom, and he kept on waving his hand, but his boss Lawrence Welk, an old man in doubleknit slacks and a not-quite-matching jacket, kept on ignoring him. Finally the trumpet player yelled, "Lawrence! Lawrence!" Lawrence snapped, "What?" The trumpet player said, "I have to go to the bathroom." Said Lawrence: "You've known about this rehearsal since last Friday!"

How did Lawrence Welk, a scrawny guy from a sod house in North Dakota, rise from such humble beginnings to make $25 million a year and enjoy such absolute tyranny over the bladders of trumpet players?

Like most tyrants, Lawrence started out with no money and no social connections. He was the sixth child of eight, "the smallest, skinniest, homeliest member" of the family, born to strict German immigrant parents. He never completed fourth grade. Lawrence shares many attributes with that other small, homely German possessed by a vision, Adolf Hitler, though the Maestro was positive and cheerful and fond of God while the feurher was rather lugubrious and didn't like God one bit. Plus Lawrence didn't have anybody killed. But they both loved music—Hitler was called a sissy because he loved Wagner's motifs so much he would hum them to himself in their entirety (he knew the librettos word for word). And though Welk delighted in consuming animal flesh and Hitler didn't, both men adored sweets, refused alcohol, slept only a few hours each night, and would not suffer poor grooming. Both were strict, demanding extreme loyalty, and were very into the idea of family. Each was a national father figure (though Hitler never fathered an actual family, and Lawrence, father of three children, worked so hard and toured so often he hardly ever saw them).

Both had a mania for documentation. The prose of both is excruciatingly detailed. They were heavily into repetition. Hitler outlined his plans in *Mein Kampf*; Lawrence shared, in every one of his books, "Our Plan"—sometimes called the Family Plan or Youth Opportunity Plan. Hitler said if you want to drive a point home, repeat it over and over. That's what Lawrence did. Instead of one accordion, Lawrence would have three accordion players playing at once. Instead of having one set of twins singing, he'd have two. What makes both men extraordinary is they made their vision come true for the whole world.

Lawrence's vision was hard work and a pleasant appearance. "Work—plain, hard, unadulterated work—is the very essence of life . . . sheer hard, persistent, dogged, untiring day-after-day work!" In Lawrence's world, the music must be pleasant, kept simple "at all costs," and performed by smiling men and lovely ladies who were never late. Lawrence could see the pleasant side of *anything*. "Calcutta," a free-wheeling, toe-tapping big dance hit, is actually a land of horror, so impoverished that every morning at sunrise there are fresh dead bodies on Beggars' Road. With his indomitable will and hard work, Lawrence Welk brought his pleasant vision into the living rooms of millions of Americans every Saturday night.

Perhaps if Hitler's home life had been more like Welk's, he wouldn't have let himself be deterred from his early pursuit of the artist's life and would've stayed out of politics. *Nothing* could keep Lawrence from *his* music.

When Lawrence's parents immigrated to America, they brought with them only two possessions: a Bible and an accordion. By the tender age of three, Lawrence could quote the one and play the other. At twenty-one, he learned English, bought a rhinestone-studded accordion, and, as Lawrence Welk & His Hotsy Totsy Boys, set out to conquer America. Initially, America didn't show any sign of being thrilled at his arrival. Times were tough. One time Lawrence had nothing to eat for two days except pickles. But with tenacity, Lawrence and his little orchestra did win the country over. Now a tougher task lay in store for Mr. Music Maker: to conquer the heart of the serious young nurse who'd caught his eye, Fern.

She rejected all his advances. He finally snagged her by arranging to have surgery he didn't need at the hospital where she worked. The unnecessary procedure caused him to hemorrhage. Through a mouthful of blood he told her how sweet she was. She was charmed. They were married at 5:30 A.M. Then they had doughnuts.

How do I know all this? Some of it came from watching *The Lawrence Welk Show*, some of it from his books. Lawrence has written several books, and they're all autobiographies. In *Wunnerful, Wunnerful* he calls his coworkers, family members and brief encounters "lovely" or "trim" every other page, and then on every *other* page he complains furiously about child labor laws and how stupid they are. Weird. In *My America, Your America*, Mr. Welk *will* share his message with you, with enthusiastically titled chapters like "Work!" and the ominous "God's Laws." *Ah-One, Ah-Two!* deals more with the subject of naps. Much of Lawrence's life has become common knowledge. People from all walks of life have a Lawrence Welk story to tell, whether they like it or not.

I first saw the show at the age of ten during a weekly visit with my mother to her classy quadriplegic friend, Mrs. McCooey. The atmosphere in that house was very restrained. There was a constant underlying battle of wills going on between Mrs. McCooey and her fat, low-class live-in housekeeper, Mrs. Taggart. For example, Mrs. McCooey wanted Mrs. Taggart to use plastic ties to close the trash bags, a method she believed left more room for garbage, thus saving pennies every week and dollars every year. It was Mrs. Taggart's choice to tie the bag with its own sides, and then lie and say she'd used the plastic ties. Ultimately, Mrs. McCooey's spies would find out and there would be a fight. But no matter how hateful her sentiments, Mrs. McCooey always kept her voice low and her language clean, which really infuriated the rowdy Mrs. Taggart. You could sometimes hear her grumbling vague, obscene threats in her room over the soaps and *The Price Is Right* playing on her itty-bitty black-and-white TV. Mrs. Taggart's choice in television programming only proved to Mrs. McCooey what a hussy the housekeeper was. On Mrs. McCooey's big color TV were permitted only the news and *Lawrence Welk*.

I couldn't understand how Mrs. McCooey could believe the show to be so wholesome or why my mother and Mrs. Taggart found it boring. To me, the constant, ultra-close-ups of moist-lipped, moist-eyed, soft-bosomed lady singers lined up side by side in matching outfits like chickens to be plucked were an open call to perversion.

Mrs. McCooey died, and I forgot about the evil Maestro for ten years until a man I'd set my sights on was somehow, somewhere, finding the fortitude to resist my seduction. I was quite depressed about that, and soothed myself by eating king-sized Chunky bars, getting drunk and then doing aerobics to Michael Jackson, and getting very thrilled by Raymond Chandler books. (One cover is a close-up of a guy getting murdered by way of a loose bedspring smashing his face to bits. Can you believe this kind of thing is for sale in public places? It was just the kind of thing to excite miserable me.) Halfway through a six-pack I happened to turn the TV on to Lawrence Welk, and the show's exotic magic struck me in the same way it had over a decade earlier, only harder, because now my unhappiness was making my fantasies even crueler and dirtier than usual, and Lawrence's extra-sweet girls were perfect fodder for my terrible desires.

During their marathon donation drive, the Public Broadcasting System would play Lawrence Welk, their most popular show, back to back for a solid week. So, there I sat in a football shirt and under-wear in my unmade bed with my beer and aspirin and chicken noo-dle soup and my broken heart, glued to the TV set for the entire week. Go out in the sunshine and listen to the birds? Nah. I was en-tranced, caught up in the queerly masculine, female-adoring mis-ogynistic, sexlessly sexful world of *The Lawrence Welk Show.*

Not much in the world could've gotten me more excited at that moment than watching those dozens of unnaturally well-scrubbed middle-aged men subjugated into wearing cherry and baby blue suits, hairsprayed caps of hair and perpetual smiles, lined up under a bigger-than-life, lit-up Geritol sign (a sponsor); little could've thrilled me more than fantasizing about what sort of undecorous de-sires lay just behind the placid, obsessedly regulated angel faces of "Lawrence's beautiful girls" while down below, ancients in wigs, with their arms around each other, moved slowly, and bubbles floated by. Fellini, Buñuel—everyone knew that was *art.* What Lawrence was doing was real life, and no one but me, I felt, knew the true nature of it all—the secret message being broadcast to mil-lions of totally unsuspecting old ladies.

Lawrence calls the men on his show his "Musical Kids." These forty-year-old kids fall into one of two categories: creepy or weepy. Leading the "weepy" category would be Joe Feeney, the Irish singer (always referred to by Lawrence as "our Irish soprano")—forever near tears, looking off in every ballad as if to his wee, green, lost country. Woe! The six-foot-five religious blond, Tom Netherton, was the leader of the "creepy" pack. Lawrence was truly in awe of Tom's handsomeness, always talking about it before and after Tom's songs. But that smile on such an immobile face, enclosed in hair never changed by time, was somehow disturbing—the teeth were just too big, and the gentle curve of the lips creeped me out. Eternally happy dancer Bobby Burgess, a former Mouseketeer, was another chill-ingly wooden "creepy" one. He looked like that secretly murderous puppet in *Magic*. Musical director/conductor George Cates, a man of otherwise unremarkable appearance, was the third "creep" who liked to demonstrate his large and frightening teeth.

I believe it was fear that caused those scary, abnormal, ever-present grins—these men were running scared. Lawrence never gave anyone a contract and was always firing people if they slipped up in any way. What kind of job is an old, fired, semi-popular tap dancer going to find? Poor Barney, a trombone player who'd been with Lawrence for twenty-five years, was fired for being too fat. The rest of the Musical Family begged Lawrence to reconsider, but the Maestro felt he had to be firm—he didn't want to set a dangerous precedent, or the entire orchestra might start getting fat! Barney begged to be given another chance, promising to lose weight, so Lawrence relented. Sort of. Barney would be kept on a week-by-week basis—as long as he lost a few pounds each week, he could stay. Barney broke down and cried in gratitude. Lawrence shamelessly relates in one of his books how week by week Barney would say "Looka here, Boss!" showing how much extra room there was in his pants' waistband—room for a finger, then for two fingers, and eventually for Barney's whole meaty fist.

Lawrence's "little girls" were fired, too, usually under murky circumstances. It was never clear, for instance, whether Alice Lon, a nervous Champagne Lady whose hands were forever cracked and bleeding, quit or was fired, or why. What we do know is this: one day Alice's neckline was too low; another day she disagreed with Lawrence about a song; next day, she was gone. Natalie Nevins, upon being fired for being tardy (supposedly due to illness), baked Lawrence a batch of blueberry muffins—he ate the muffins but remained firm, and she remained jobless. When Lawrence wasn't firing, he was promising to fire. In every second or third chapter of any of Lawrence's books, there's a pretty lady in Lawrence's office, crying copious tears, trying to get her job back. Lawrence has quite a knack for describing a woman in tears, begging.

Showing too much leg or having too-pointy boobs (or is that t-w-o pointy boobs?) was sure to land one of Lawrence's "little girls" out the door on her too-much bottom. But in spite of these potential sexiness-eradicating precautions—or because of the fervor with which these precautions were taken—the viewer cannot (or at least *I* cannot) think of anything but "oral sex . . . oral sex" upon seeing these girls. They have more makeup on than any prostitute I've ever seen—gobby lip gloss and blue sparkly eyeshadow. Then there's a soft lens on the camera so the gobby lips are even gobbier and the eyes are like shining stars; ultra-close-ups of lips and well-plucked eyebrows raised high above big, wide eyes, wordlessly beckoning, "Come be sucked by me now." Lawrence insisted on the girls wearing empire dresses: those high-waisted, flowing garments that cover its wearer from neck to wrist to feet, tight in only one area: up against the breasts. So all you can focus on are those moist lips and eyes and those melons—surrounded by a halo of feather boas, twinkling tiaras and drifting cardboard clouds in pleasant pastels suspended by threads. From between the lips drift up angelic voices describing hand-holding and home, sweet home. The face takes up the entire screen—staring, smiling, eyes moist, cheeks round . . . the camera pans a bit; the back is straight, the well-covered body is gently swaying. . . .

And then there are the group shots; eight or nine women in their thirties who all look alike (most of them are sisters, or at least in-laws), wearing matching outfits, sitting on a haystack or a cardboard caboose, with their arms about each other's waists, all gently swaying and smiling and gazing and singing sweetly about love. It's enough to make me feel like Attila the Hun, raring to go plunder!

The six Semonski sisters, Lawrence reveals in *My America, Your America*, did a lot of "jiggling." He was always having to tell them in his sternest voice, "Stand still!" at which point all six would collapse into each other's arms, giggling and embarrassed. Just then Lawrence mentions the myriad child labor laws he "literally ached"* to change in order to work with a "freer hand." Could Lawrence really be so innocent he didn't notice the sexual overtones to his choice of words—all that jiggling and giggling and aching? I'm sure he *didn't* notice. But *I* did!

Lawrence's only visible purpose on his show (besides introducing the Mexican singer as "the lovely little Mexican songstress I found in Escondido" every single time) is to "conduct" the orchestra of accordian players, violinists and tranglers. Lawrence does this by walking around with a vacant but joyful/hopeful expression on his face, conductor's baton drooping forgotten from his hand. After his retirement at age seventy-nine, when Lawrence did the "wraparounds"—remarks to open and close the reruns—a golf club took the place of the conductor's baton: dangling irrelevantly from Lawrence's hand as he walked around and smiled with unfocused eyes into the camera.

That's how Lawrence met *everyone*—by chance at golf tournaments. God knows what all these chanteuses and trombone players were doing out playing golf, but there they were, and when they spotted Lawrence, they would just break into song or whip out a tape of themselves playing xylophone, and Lawrence would hire them. Either that, or he met them in restaurants—there the Welks would be, quietly eating rump roast, when a man at the next table would spontaneously break into "My Country 'Tis of Thee" with spoon and fork on tabletop, and a new member of The Lawrence Welk Musical Family would be born. One aspiring artiste—a whistler—auditioned for Lawrence in a public bathroom.

Once you join Lawrence's Family, you're in for life—even if you're fired! It's a cult! You keep appearing at Lawrence Welk tributes and hosting reruns of the show every year for the rest of your life, and write books about the show, and just sit around remembering what it was like being on the show. Some of the members of The Musical Family went on to form their own entertainment tours, in which they carry on the spirit of Lawrence Welk, and talk all interview long about how wonderful Lawrence is, every chance they get to be interviewed. Natalie Nevins (the fired muffin-baker) today has this to say: "Meeting Mr. Welk was the most wonderful event of my entire life!" When one considers all the events of a lifetime—love, marriage, sex, childbirth, travel—one is very impressed, wondering just what a meeting with Mr. Welk could be like.

I wish I had met him. Like Hitler, Walt Disney and Henry Ford, Lawrence Welk was one of the powerful men of our century who made his private dream a reality for everybody. He rose from humble beginnings—why, his family didn't even have indoor plumbing—with his dream steadfast in his mind. He guarded that dream fiercely, allowing no deviation, nurturing it with his whole life, until that dream came true in a BIG way. Millions of viewers were enthralled by the dream of this skinny little guy with a ridiculous accent. The dream: extreme close-ups of *nice* people singing nice songs and dancing anachronistic dances against insanely cheerful backdrops. It's a beautiful dream! And hovering at the edge of this dream come true is Mr. Music Maker, smiling benevolently—and promising with that smile to reward those who please him and to get rid of anyone, immediately and without mercy, who messes the dream up in even the littlest way. One can't be too careful about one's dreams.

A Visit to

the Sadistic

Beauty Parlor

My youthful passion was playing the victim in
Rescue Squad practice days. If you think
beauty salons are exciting, imagine being
wrapped up, splintered, eyes bandaged, on a
stretcher, by several people at once.

> —*Nell Zink*

She hurt me. She hurt my feelings and she
hurt my scalp. I've never felt so helpless.
Elba—Elba The Bloodcurdling.

> —*me (Lisa)*

In ancient times, having one's hair done was an event, complete with a dozen or so maids and family members milling about, life-and-death secrets, animal fat for hair grease, and pain. Maids in charge of hairdressing were beaten with mirrors, poked with hairpins and otherwise abused if even one curl stuck out wrong. After a day-long hairdressing session, a woman would write her friends and relatives big, long letters all about it. Back then, people *cared* about their hair. Even as late as the 1930s, when a woman left the hairdresser's, it was with puffy eyes from the chemicals, a blistered forehead or even a fever . . . and the most beautiful 'do! I was in search of that mood.

I had never found it growing up in New Hampshire. There, I went to Becky The Silent (my secret nickname for her). Becky and I were the only ones at the Fifth Street Beauty Salon under sixty-five. All the patrons' scalps showed through their sparse hair. Though Becky was only in her thirties, I believe being surrounded by so much oldness had petrified her soul, and she just had nothing to say. Mostly everyone was silent, hypnotized by the rhythmic snipping of clippers, the gentle rush of rinse water and the airy drone of hair dryers. Conversation, when there was any, revolved around department store sales and dead husbands. No one beat anyone with hand mirrors.

It took a move to San Francisco to find the hairdresser of my dreams: Elba. If this was Salem in the 1690s, Elba would have been burned at the stake. In the late twentieth century, though, she owned a beauty salon on 23rd Street. Only the Mission District of San Francisco, with its filthy, dangerous, glamorous streets, could raise a wildcat like my Elba . . . Elba, She-Beast of the Cosmeticians. That fateful day in October when I left my messy little apartment to go meet the hairdresser of my dreams was not a normal brisk autumn day. It was exceedingly humid, as if the atmosphere were made up of thousands of clammy hands touching me all over, hurrying me on to meet my destiny.

I knew Elba's Salon was the one for me when I saw the faded early 1980s posters in the window. No one's known how to do hair since then. Tony salons won't streak my hair the way I need it done. They say the old way is too damaging, and now they use tinfoil wraps and gentle bleaches and it's really boring. I don't care for the new look: natural, subtle. When I get my hair streaked, I want it done rough! I wanna look *streaked*. So I have to seek out the sleaziest place in town, a place where beauticians haven't succumbed to hairdresser peer pressure and are still willing to destroy a few hair follicles. In San Francisco, Elba's is it. The background of the posters must once have been magenta, but were now peach with white splotches. The makeup and dye on the models were so strong in 1985 that after ten years of sun-fading, there was still more on them than on anyone walking down the street that day. Anyone, that is, except Elba herself.

I walked in, wrote my name down on the waiting list, and sat down opposite a huge plaster cast of the Crucifixion—Christ, bleeding and crying and rolling his eyes. It was a portent of things to come. Framed magazine reproductions of paintings of the agonized, dying man adorned the walls—mostly close-ups of his sweating, twisted face—and on each flat surface stood vases bursting with plastic, dusty, exotic flowers. Iron-on decals of people dancing decorated the bulgy part of every vase. Death and dancing seemed to be the motif here. In the history of the gods, Elba would represent Abraxas, the deity that embraces both light and dark, good and evil, life . . . *and death.* So ran my thoughts until they were cut short by the very alive voice of Elba: "I'm ready for you now, if you are ready for me!" This was my last chance to turn back: *Was* I ready for Elba? But Elba wasn't really asking; she was commanding. "You sit in the yellow chair now, Lisa Ann." I thought back to my safe, gentle, silent Becky, took a deep breath, and moved to the chair indicated.

"My name is just Lisa, not Lisa Ann," I corrected.

Elba said, "To me, you're Lisa Ann." Well!

Elba put a plastic covering over my body and tied a towel around my neck. "That's not too tight, is it?" It was, but I didn't say so. I wasn't about to argue with Elba. Elba was around forty-five and wore that amazing, greasy blue eyeshadow that no one's put on since 1979 (and only waitresses and fourteen-year-old girls on the wrong side of the law wore it even then), tons of greasy black eyeliner, fake eyelashes, cake foundation and rouge. In a way, Elba's face was pretty; in another way, it was the spitting image of General Noriega. Elba was thickset and rather tall for a Mexican. Her flesh was the color and consistency of tofu; her figure a masterpiece of rubber stays. One could, if one squinted, just make out the outline of a fierce brassiere, girdle and control pantyhose. I found it comforting to see Elba in such command of her physical form, squishing it into whatever form she chose. At the same time, the absolute mystery as to its natural shape sent a tingle of curiosity down my spine: who knew what shape it would take when released from its many bindings? I looked into the mirror at myself in the plastic and Elba standing behind me, her blonded hair in curlers. I said, "We're having our hair done at the same time." She said, "Lisa Ann, I'll tell you something now. Every morning I come in here and put my hair in curlers, and when the curlers come out and I leave here, I'm ready for *anything* that might happen." Wow! Elba held up a plastic cap with pinprick holes in it and a sharp metal instrument that looked like that tool used to make latch-hook rugs. "I'm going to put this cap on your head and be jabbing your scalp and pulling your hair through tiny holes for the next hour. But first I give your hair a good comb-out. It's going to be painful. Do you want some Tylenol?" No, thanks. I wanted to remember every detail.

Elba was lifting my hair up and down haphazardly, like she was trying to decide where to start combing, but really she was ignoring me, engrossed by the tale being told by a waiting patron, Kitty, about her husband needing a liver and lung transplant. I was engrossed, too, since I'd never even heard of a lung transplant before. So were the other two ladies in the shop: a second, older hairdresser, Millie, who was either black, Asian or Hispanic, and her customer, Mirtha, a Hispanic woman, around forty years old, with ten or twelve beauty magazines sliding around on her lap.

Elba, running her fingers kindly through my hair, said to Kitty, "You know, sometimes they never find a liver or lung to use. Those organs are good only two, three months—after that they just throw them away, and people do not donate like they used to. How is your blood pressure, Kitty?"

"Bad. Way up, way up."

"At least you're thin."

"Not thin," Kitty contradicted. "I'm fat!"

"Artichokes are good for your blood pressure," advised Mirtha, and I thought this to be bad advice, because artichokes, especially soaked in butter as they usually are, seem very fatty. But I buttoned my lip, content to wait for my hair treatment and to let these diseases follow their own destiny.

Millie asked how Kitty's daughter was.

"She want to quit her job because she work with human tissue," said Kitty. "She wonder if she is already infected and will have a deformed baby."

"Why's she still work?" asked Mirtha.

"The reason she keep on working is she is putting her husband through medical school."

"I just hope he don't leave her the day he graduate," Elba pronounced, looking mournful, but I believe she was actually quite enjoying baiting the unfortunate Kitty. No wonder Kitty's blood pressure was up—mine would be too if Elba was my friend. "They do that, you know. Leave her all alone with a deformed baby."

"He does that," Kitty said menacingly, "I bring him back—in two pieces."

"You can't trust anyone anymore," sighed Millie, "but you have to trust."

"Elba, I think I might be a redhead sometime," said Kitty.

"No, that don't look good on you. You stay with dark brown, maybe a little less dark brown."

Suddenly, Kitty was sure she wanted red hair. "No, I think I might have you make me redhead today!"

"You will hate it. You trust me, Kitty, it will look so bad and copper, like a penny. It will look horrible. You have so much chemicals in your hair already, and with your complexion. . . ." Elba let that hang in the air threateningly. Elba, it seemed, was one of those women who just *had* to disagree, even when it went against their own best interest. It appeared that Kitty was one of those women, too, for now she was vehement: "I will have red hair today, and I will look so young and beautiful. I need a change for my happiness, and I will be a redhead!" She scrambled to her feet like a bull who has spied the red cape waving. At the start, Kitty had only been contemplating changing her hair color someday. Now she was ferociously going ahead with a plan that was probably a bad one, just to spite Elba. And Elba was near to losing a customer, maybe giving a woman with high blood pressure a heart attack, but that wasn't about to stop her from being mean! If those two had been monsters in an old Japanese movie, Tokyo would have been saved— only because the monsters wiped each other out through sheer orneriness.

Kitty fumed out the door. She could have been off to get her hair dyed red by a more normal human being than Elba, but I thought it more likely she would just walk off her rage and come back. The battle had been drawn. She couldn't just walk away; she must make Elba give in and dye her hair red.

As soon as Kitty was gone, Mirtha told us that the husband was having an affair! Imagine that, he needs a lung and liver transplant and he's having sneaky sex with somebody. It's true, I thought, you can't trust anyone anymore.

Two boys walked by. "Look at their pants halfway down their business!" Mirtha said. "That's disgusting." We all agreed it was disgusting, and Elba told Millie to lock the door.

"They don't have no school," said Elba, "they don't have no job. They suppose to have something to do. It used to be nice to be Latino, but now. . . ."

"Now they kill somebody," said Mirtha.

"Fourteen, fifteen years old," said Millie sadly.

"They don't have anything else to do," Elba said.

At first sighting of the boys, Elba had stopped lifting and letting fall my hair, instead coming at me with a comb in her hand. As if to demonstrate what should be done to boys who aren't in school or at work, she jabbed the comb into my scalp again and again, just about piercing it.

Elba's mother named her well. The House of Elba is much like the island of Elba. It too was a bleak, cruel place for punishment, except here donor lungs rot, husbands leave their young wives and deformed babies, and Elba's many-toothed comb is an instrument of retribution against all injustice. And for some reason my tender scalp seemed to be the spot where that vengeful woman believed those injustices were hiding. Napoleon was sent to Elba for failing as an emperor; my punishment was for forsaking the hairdresser I knew and trusted (Becky) in search of thrills. Under Elba's punishing comb, I was getting all the thrills I wanted—and many more.

The discussion moved onto Mexican nationalists who steal luggage. These people, judging by the increased pain I felt under Elba's brittle comb, make her even madder than boys with their pants down around their bum. "The little fish always have to bite the tail of the big fish!" concluded Elba with fury.

"It's so easy to steal," said Millie, even more sadly than before, "because people trust."

"You have a big head," Elba suddenly announced, loudly. "I will have to get the *big* cap for you." She was talking to me. I looked around—everyone else had normal-sized heads, and they were all staring at me. My head's not that big, I told myself. It's only because I'm skinny that it looks big. I considered my head in the mirror and thought, Elba is a bad woman.

That bad woman screwed the cap onto my head as if she were scrubbing a tub made deliberately grimy by inconsiderate bathers, and set to spearing my scalp so viciously with the latch-hook rug tool that I began to feel queasy. I wondered in earnest why I had come here. The ladies with normal-sized heads continued discussing untrustworthy men and deformed babies, and as I had just become pregnant by a man I'd known for only a few weeks, their talk was making me even queasier. Then Mirtha began telling a story about a woman they all knew who had a baby even though the doctors told her not to, and it was born with a cord coming out of its head: "So the baby had an operation and was all right, but the doctors said to Joy, 'Now you *really* better not have another baby.' But the first baby was a girl"—Mirtha paused and looked at everyone meaningfully—"so Joy did have another baby, and this one was a boy"—she passed around an even more meaningful look—"and he was born retarded!"

Millie clicked her tongue and shook her head, and Elba picked up the story: "Well, Joy and her husband fought all the time about the retarded boy, until in the end they divorced."

Millie clicked again, and it occurred to me that these women had probably told each other this story many times before.

Elba had been going at my scalp for an hour and was only done pulling the hair through one side of the cap. "You're making a face," she noted. "Do you usually cry when you have your hair done?"

"No!" I said defiantly.

"Ho!" Elba chortled. I wanted to rip my cap off and run out the door, flee cruel Elba. I wanted to throw the cap down on the floor and stomp on it, grind it beneath my heel and say something nasty to Elba. Maybe tell her that no one wears rouge like that anymore. But I was caught, caught in the spell of the hairdresser. Time came in waves, past and present overlapping. In my ears echoed the whispers of gossips hundreds of years old; the sweet and pungent sting of hairspray drifted back into the lead derivatives used by citizens of the ancient Nile (which caused birth defects and early death!) and back again into modern ozone-destroying Aquanet; and my body was encircled by ghosts holding hairpins and viles of crushed newt's guts—all that has been hairdressing over the centuries now had me pinned in my yellow chair. I could not escape my fate: like all my ancestors throughout the ages I must sit here under the instrument of torture, which is, in the year of our Lord 1994, a hair hook.

Mirtha was describing the operation performed to remove the cord from the baby girl's head when suddenly my stomach broke the spell: I leapt out of my chair and yelled, "Where's the bathroom?"

Elba pointed silently, and everyone looked with interest at me for the first time, probably wondering if I had an inflamed bowel that I might, with proper coaxing, tell them all about. I felt six eyes follow me into the bathroom.

The instant I was alone in there, I felt better. When I came back out and sat in my yellow chair, Elba tried to pretend I'd been crying. I said, "No I wasn't. I just felt nauseous."

"I don't believe you," said that nasty old beast.

"I'm pregnant," I told them all, displaying my one and only trump card. I knew now that I couldn't just have the fun side of a visit to the sadistic beauty salon. This wasn't turning out anything like my simple fantasies. I knew now that my battle lines, like Kitty's, were drawn. It was a contest of wills, and I suddenly felt confident. I felt up to the fight. I was not about to let hairdresser Elba, nor her old cronies, break *my* spirit. I knew the news of my pregnancy would get 'em. It did. Three heads bounced up.

"You don't look fat," said Elba suspiciously, unable to believe her good fortune: new tales of constipation, fatigue and varicose veins at least, and maybe even something special—perhaps a cyst found on the tiny kidneys via sonogram.

"I'm fatter than I was three months ago," I said in answer to Elba's challenge.

She suddenly changed tact. "Would you like a glass of water?"

But I wasn't falling for her ruse—I knew she was buttering me up so I'd give them details on my nausea, "pink toothbrush," etc. I may be new to this game, but I learn fast. I wouldn't tell them anything!

I could feel everyone waiting. I owed them a pregnancy story. I felt the pressure and started to sweat. Elba wasn't touching my hair; nobody moved. I did not know if I could hold out.

Just then an old man arrived at the door, breaking the tension. Millie unlocked it for him, he came in, sat down, didn't speak to anyone, and no one spoke to him. No one cut his hair either. "He's ninety years old!" Elba yelled in my ear, as if to prove how completely deaf the old guy was. "His back is going out on him! He's traveling to El Salvador by car! I wouldn't go to El Salvador under the best circumstances, definitely not at ninety years old with a bad back!"

Why was he here? Eventually he just got up and left.

Elba looked at me in a new way and said, "Do you dance?"

I told her I was taking ballroom dancing lessons.

"Lisa Ann, I tell you something: no one need lessons." All of her attention was on me now, as if there were just the two of us in the room. "To me, dancing is like eating—you just do it with your body.

I see a dance once, and I can do it. I have my own dance room in my house—The Florida Room. It has a tiled floor. I can dance to everything—salsa, rap, music from all over the world. Everything but Chinese—Chinese music does not turn me on. My husband, for his sixty-fifth birthday I bought him a belly dancer. She was American; she had the technique—she had obviously taken all the lessons. She had the body; she had the jewels on her fingers. . . . But my husband said, 'You didn't need to spend eighty-five dollars on her—you're a better belly dancer than her.' And I am!"

Suddenly, I thought Elba was wonderful. Elba yanked the last bits of my hair through the microscopic cap holes and turned me over to two assistants who appeared from nowhere. They took me to the back of the room and applied bluish bleach paste with brushes to my hair. It felt like dog paws patting gently at either side of my head. The bleach made a tingling sound like soft snow falling on the previous night's snow crust. I felt like I was falling asleep to a lullaby.

As neither assistant spoke English, they had to push or pull my head to get it into the angles they needed. Some bleach got on my cheek. I tried to explain that I needed a washcloth, and the two assistants went over to Elba, who scolded them in Spanish for getting bleach on my face. Elba not only refused to hand me the warm, wet washcloth so I could wash myself, but insisted on scrubbing not only the cheek where the bleach landed, but my entire face and neck, too. I felt clean! Elba wouldn't let the other two touch me after that. She washed my hair three times. Then she ripped the cap off. She worked silently now, and gently, combing through my hair, which was horribly snarled by the bleach and the cap.

"That shampoo smells so good," I said.

Elba showed me the bottle. "It is made with human placenta, that make it so strong." She sold me a bottle—$16. Total debauchery—rubbing human meat into my hair and paying ten times the normal shampoo price to do it. In the old days in Rome, before going on a fancy date one would have one's scalp rubbed with the body of a boiled lizard. Such unusual expressions of carnivorous behavior in beauty parlors!

Elba squirted mousse into her hand. I said, "Oh no, no mousse. I don't like sticky hair." Instead of wiping it off on a towel, she used her assistant's luxurious long hair!

My new hair color surprised me. She had done it the Mexican way—very light blonde all along the part, as if the sun had beat down on my head. (Anglo-Saxons tend to apply the bleach heaviest to the bangs and the hair framing the face—as if one were holding a flashlight under the chin.) Since it turned out a lot lighter than the picture I had brought in, Elba offered to put some brown streaks back in next Tuesday. I thought it looked fine, but if Elba wanted to see me again, I wasn't going to say no. I began making plans to get a manicure, too . . . we'd be holding hands.

My manicure daydreams were interrupted by the abrupt actions of Elba. My entire visit had been a cycle of pleasant dreams and harsh reality. Despite my protestations that I didn't need absolutely dry hair, Elba was sticking me under a hair dryer, and turned it to hot and high. So hot and high I could see but not hear what happened next to the little boy, maybe two years old, brought in by his grandma for a haircut.

At first the young man was brave and close-mouthed under Elba's leaping shears. But I could see his face in the mirror, and I saw panic building in his rolling eyes. His mouth began to tremble. I knew how he felt. Elba's mouth remained tightly closed. She made no move to comfort him, nor did she relax her wild snipping one bit, as if she found it perfectly normal for someone to be terrified under her care. And then, when Elba turned on the electric razor, I could see the boy was sobbing. His grandma's face remained impassive. Millie and Mirtha rose, as if unaware of their actions, and drifted like ghouls nearer to the boy. Lucky for Elba that they were there, because the boy had truly panicked now, and was using every ounce of his two-year-old's strength to hurtle himself out of that chair and away from Elba and her buzzing razor. It took Millie and Mirtha plus the grandma to hold the boy down while Elba took a mercilessly long time to shave just a tiny bit of hair.

I hated Elba at that moment, and every other woman in there. My hair was light now, but my soul was black with fury.

The boy's cut was done. The grandma took him away, and Millie sat Mirtha down under the dryer next to mine. Millie with her sympathetic tongue-clicking and her sad eyes, Mirtha with her juicy gossip and beauty magazines and her friendly artichoke advice—these two women had just held down a child, barely more than a baby, while Elba terrified him. I felt like I had seen something horrible, really horrible. Maybe I'm making a big deal out of a very ordinary episode in a child's life—his first haircut—but the expression on those women's faces as they held this child down was true evil. They showed him no mercy. My day at the sadistic hairdresser wasn't funny anymore.

Millie checked Mirtha's hair and it was dry. I had been under the machine longer, but Elba didn't care that I was dry and hot and mad—she just left me there. Millie brushed out Mirtha's hairdo and the two went off together, arm in arm. It was just Elba and me now. I was scared.

But my fear came to an anticlimatic end with the arrival of another patron. Elba motioned her into the yellow chair I had thought of as mine. "Now I'll never get out from under this dryer," I fumed. "I'm forgotten!"

But in a few minutes, Elba lifted the dryer off my hair, fluffed it up a bit with her masculine, tofu-y hands, took my money and turned her back on me. I couldn't believe it was ending like this. I had gone through so many emotions, there was so much to say. I turned and left.

A month later, I returned to New Hampshire, but three thousand miles couldn't get Elba and the little boy out of my mind. I was still mostly mad and disgusted at Elba and her cronies, but with the distance there was a little fondness and excitement mixed in my memories, too.

Now, a year later, laying against my pillows, safe, surrounded by books and pictures and paintings of the things that I love, I'll admit it—I like Elba. She's wild! I thought I hated her while the young boy and I were in her grasp, but I simply misidentified the never before visited realm of pleasure her sturdy, square hands were pulling and pushing me into.

The advent of the computer, the microwave and the TV have created a world where we work alone, eat alone and laugh alone. TV is not a bad thing (I love mine so much!); nevertheless, today's concentration on the brain has made us forget we are human *animals,* and we get lonely. We miss the herd. The beauty parlor is one of the few cultural islands left where humans teem. The beauty parlor is where everything interesting in life, everything alluring, is experienced firsthand, physically, rather than through the spectrum of some screen or another. It's so emotional in there! And all these people are stroking your hair. The atmosphere is centuries old, yet very *now* too. Elba is not bound to our technological era. Were Armageddon to befall us tomorrow and wipe out electricity and organized delivery systems, Elba would still have a job. Her gossip would take the place of Associated Press Wire Services. Instead of using bleach in a bottle, she'd squeeze the juice out of an unfortunate iguana directly onto her customer's hair. A woman like Elba finds a way. She is the eternal queen of the hairdressers, in all her cruel and knowing glory.

A Place Where Only Girls Can Go: To the Gynecologist

My masturbation fantasy throughout my
entire teens was that Devo was my
gynecologist. They were behind a window,
monitoring my pulse rate with equipment.
They looked so scientific.

—*Dame Darcy*

$\mathcal{R}$**ecently I asked** a bunch of people about what turns them on. An astonishing zero percent answered "going to the hairdresser or the doctor." Those doctor/hairdresser situations—where the patient/client has to act all businesslike and brave, and hide the sensuality sprung by hot, manipulating fingers, cold stethoscopes, hot curlers and staccato commands followed by gentle reassurances—get me feeling pretty romantic.

How many people are allowed to touch your hair, your neck, your ears? Three only: your lover, your doctor and your beautician. The situation is so intimate, yet decorum requires you to remain poker-faced, no matter how claustrophobic, tickled or excited you feel. I read a book about a man who had hemophilia or some disease since childhood that required much pestering by doctors. Because this went on during his adolescent sexual awakening, he came to associate his erection with doctors' visits, and as an adult he got that same thrill by jabbing needles into himself or getting his girlfriend to do it. That would never work for me. It is the *illicit* pleasure caused by *necessary* procedures performed by *removed* professionals that gets my temperature rising. It is a rare occasion when I don't lustily enjoy a doctor's visit or a trip to the beauty parlor. (I like grueling school exams, too; there the same thing is done to the pupil's mind as is done to the patient's body. I even get excited when the census bureau comes to visit.)

All of this might go back to when, as a young girl, I would fake being asleep so that my undemonstrative father would pick me up and carry me to bed. I believe we enjoyed that ritual equally—he was a loving father who just felt awkward showing it. I bet he was happy for the utilitarian excuse to hold his little girl in his arms. Too, I am sometimes positive my doctor or beautician is secretly enjoying doing things to me as much as I am secretly enjoying having them done. Those sly devils!

The loss of control is what most women hate about going to the gynecologist. Everyone knows about in-control pleasures, like when you finally get your own car and you slip down the highway. It's just as pleasurable, however, to utterly lose control—like hanging upside-down in that cage on The Zipper at the amusement park and screaming, "Aaa! Let me down! I hate this! Stop!" even though you know no way is that man fifty feet below with the control stick in his hand gonna stop The Zipper. Only people don't usually *realize* they're enjoying themself just then. A gynecological exam is the latter type of pleasure—the hard to relax, absolutely thrilling, nearly impossible to recognize as pleasure type of pleasure.

Most girls are horrified (or pretend to be) when that annual visit to the gynecologist rolls around. They say they feel violated. They say they dread having their naked legs open and their feet locked in stirrups while someone fully clothed shines a hot light on their most secret spot and sticks cold metal instruments into it. For a certain kind of girl, the kind who would ride The Zipper ten times in a row, a visit to the gynecologist is like Christmas—it only happens once a year and she gets lots of things she wants. She skips to the clinic while visions of speculums dance in her head.

The first enjoyable part of the gynecological exam is filling out forms in the waiting room. It's very formal and ceremonial. With a serious face, the receptionist hands you a clipboard with pages and pages of questions. Those doctors are interested in things no one else knows: your every venereal disease ever, how many people you've done it with, whether you ever had an abortion, the cancer in your family tree, past and present drug use, your true weight. . . . You imagine well-groomed, clean-hand doctors in white coats gathered around your forms, discussing you, knowing so much about you, knowing whatever they want! About the doctors, you know nothing. And never will. They are invisible, impersonal, informed. You are at their mercy. They can order whatever tests they want for you. They could even make jokes behind your back about your sexual history.

If you're a man, perhaps it doesn't seem that appealing. But I have this theory that every woman, despite her own unique personality, is part submissive masochistic exhibitionist. And a trip to the gynecologist answers every one of those hidden needs!

After completing the forms and handing them to the receptionist, the patient is guided by an underling to a small, simple room, where her pulse, weight and a blood sample are taken. These nurses are always young and nervous, and worry so much over the patient's comfort they can't concentrate on the task at hand—especially the blood-taking part. Their fumbly caution is a delicious juxtaposition to the sexy, forceful probing by the doctor soon to come.

Some women don't like male gynecologists because they're too "rough and cranky." I happen to like rough and cranky men. But I prefer female doctors because I am fascinated by female flesh. I don't want to be a lesbian and do all the lesbian things—like wear a rainbow pin and read up on women's voting history, if that's what they do, and have my mother worry about not getting any more grandkids out of me—and yet I do wish to be felt up by a lady. So being stroked in my three extra hot spots for half an hour by a woman in white for health reasons is the perfect experience.

I have another theory. It's about lesbianism. My theory is: women are just cuter than men, so it's natural that women would be attracted to other women. If you're a woman and you go to second base with another woman, you're just expressing normal artistic appreciation for beauty. If you go to third base, you might be one or you might not. The only sure way to know is if you get a home run, which I've never done, so I believe I'm hetero. A sexologist might not be swayed by my theory, but it seems very reasonable to me when I'm naked with my feet in stirrups while a learned lady feels me up.

The first thing the doctor does is demonstrate the proper way to do a breast self-exam, even if the patient already knows how. "You must become *intimate* with the feel of your own breasts," the doctor explains, kneading each breast in concentric circles. "This way you are best able to identify a *lump*." As the doctor's adept fingers press on and on, a big *lump* forms in my throat. One time a cute redhead doctor spent *so* long attending to my breasts—minutes and minutes of squeezing and even caressing—that I about swooned. "Your breasts are so firm and well-shaped," she commented in a friendly manner. "It must be nice to have small breasts." (She had big, soft ones herself. I could tell.) This young woman was very different from the usual stiff, prudish gynecologist; she wore gobs of juicy lip gloss, and I bet anachronistic hot curlers produced those sensual, bouncing curls in her hair. I couldn't believe my good fortune.

Next your belly is poked with the doctor's gloved finger a half-dozen times. We're getting closer. And you have to act all serious. There's a feeling of secrecy and danger, like when your boyfriend is discreetly fondling your bottom while you sit on the couch, and you're baby-sitting so you have to act like you're not excited and nothing's going on. The doctor greases up the glove while telling you she is doing so. She tells you she is going to insert a finger into your vagina to examine your cervix—"Oh," you say with studied nonchalance—and then does it. (They always describe everything they do as they do it, I guess to reassure you. It's all dirty words to me.) She shines a really hot light between your legs, and you begin to melt. Now there is a speculum in her hand. "This is going to be cold," she warns. It is. It's delightful—cold metal tube, hot bright light, hot bright you.

"Now I'm going to open the speculum. You're going to feel a little *pressure* as it gets bigger," the doctor purrs reassuringly. "Now

I'm going to take a sample of your cervix lining with this swab." The swab looks like a tiny bunny tail on the end of a stick, and she glides it through the tube until it rubs against a spot too deep inside for even the most exploratory of male members to hit.

The doctor offers to hold a mirror up so you can see your cervix through the opened speculum. Together, the lady and you observe your treasure. "Ooh, it's pink," you cry happily. It looks like the inside of a seashell, glistening with brine. Rarely has a lover's face reflected the frank and knowledgeable appreciation of your female parts as does the doctor's now. You feel very pretty.

Alas, although you feel your adventure has just begun, the doctor announces that it is now concluded. You dress and float home, dreaming of continuing the exam with someone a little less professionally removed. In your back pocket is something you stole while the good doctor was out of the room: a brand new pair of latex gloves.

Other Ladies'

Bodies

$\mathcal{I}$ **agree with Grigor Karamazov:** you can find something attractive in *any* woman. He proved he meant what he said by having sex with a retarded streetperson in front of his buddies. Unfortunately, she then got pregnant and died giving birth in a tool shed. Of course Mr. Karamazov's actions are reprehensible, but he's right. There is something attractive even in a retarded streetperson. It could be appealing because it is forbidden, or just because it's so gross and shocking to think of going through with the act— sometimes horror brings out one's sensuality, like when a couple watch a movie where somebody gets ripped apart limb from limb by a monster, then they go home and have sex. It could be there is something sinisterly exciting in taking something so helpless and innocent and stinky as a retarded streetperson. You're thinking, "I'm so bad. I'm so evil"—and then . . . what's that stirring down below? Sproing! Oh, terrible.

When riding in a car, I keep my eye out for the plain, unremarkable, quiet-looking girl moving quietly along the sidewalks. Brown hair, brown eyes, flat shoes—you know she must have some secret dirty thoughts. Vile thoughts growing like mushrooms in the dark. Unlike more ribald women, a plain woman hugs her dirty thoughts close, never letting them see the light of day . . . that's the kind of thing I wanna know!

I feel jolly when I see a sleazy woman. Silk dress or white tank top, her boobs (in the shape of triangular wedges of cheesecake or water balloons) hang out as she leans down, pretending to rebuckle her shoes. The stares collect on her skin, glowing there. She likes mischief. She enjoys making other women furious. She's bad but happy. This is her moment of glory—to show her young body and evil face and long, loose hair. Her life is on fire.

I love those black velvet paintings where the naked woman with a gleam in her eye stands half hidden in shadows, showing off her buttocks which are, without fail, as long and meaty as a horse's. Do these women really exist? I hope so. I hope they aren't all dieting and wearing long, dark, thick skirts. Perhaps they should write to me at P.O. Box 474, Dover, NH 03821.

I like skinny girls, too. They look like an airplane—all streamlined and fast. Small breasts are sweet, especially braless ones.

Most of all, I like the famous ladies. There are so many pictures of them! Reading the worst- and best-dressed issue of *People*, I feel like I used to when I'd baby-sit and, as soon as the mother would leave, I'd peek at her photo album. Below is a list of women, some famous, some not, I've had the pleasure of perusing on many occasions. Even when I hate them, it's a pleasure.

HELEN GURLEY BROWN
(The skinny old woman who ran
Cosmopolitan for about a million years)

I am terrified of this woman. She represents the dark side of skinny. There's nothing left on her but a dress, some bones, a wig and teeth—yet still she diets! What is there left to lose? She must be trying to halve her bones, get skinnier teeth. She's ninety, and she's had ninety facelifts. If you shaved the hair behind her ear I bet you'd see her chin from 1950. She is a human spider. When I found out she has a husband, I couldn't believe it. And he likes her to look like that! Someone told me he said so. To think of her *touching* him with those spider hands. . . .

JAMIE LEE CURTIS

There's only one thing I can't abide by in a lady's body, and that's a flat stomach: the Jamie Lee Curtis stomach. It looks miserly. Seeing someone fight nature so hard makes me nervous. Nature wants you to have a belly. Jamie Lee Curtis said she eats only a salad all day long. That's not right! Her belly is a part of her body she cut off on purpose, leaving the admirerer with nothing to admire between the boobs and the you-know-what. How cruel! I don't like cruel ladies. Except sometimes I do.

KATE MOSS

Kate Moss has a lovely body, and her face is both regal and fishlike. She smokes cigarettes and goes out with violent and spoiled men, yet still she appears so young and untouched. She's naturally skinny, but has a cute little pot belly. I like all her odd juxtapositions. From her interviews it seems she might be a bit dull in the brain, but so what? Lots of smart people are ugly and you still admire *them*. On *The Ricki Lake Show* audience members are always standing up to shriek self-righteously that old cliché as if they had just invented it: "IT'S WHAT'S INSIDE THAT COUNTS!" Well what about the outside, doesn't it get any credit? In *Unzipped*, Kate was the only model not constantly making up to the camera like a fool, and she didn't say one word throughout the whole movie. I read in the paper that she was having a fight with Isaac Mizrahi. I like the women who have the fights with the famous men and the bosses.

DOLLY PARTON

Dolly is another woman who embraces contradictions. She's generous yet ambitious; devoted to her husband, but she sleeps around like crazy. Not only that, she writes the most beautiful songs, and she has fifty wigs! She is Woman! On the down side, her long fake nails are grotesque. And I am worried about her—her legs and waist just keep getting skinnier and skinner. Dolly, please, quit that diet!

MARIAH CAREY

She's cute, all circles: hair in ringlets, round nose tip, round mouth, round eyes, round boobies, round hips. Elitist social commentators make fun of her because she has an eight-octave voice, as if it's some kind of trick. These are the same people that think Kate Moss must be lying when she says she eats whatever she wants, as if no one on earth is just naturally skinny or blessed with an eight-octave voice! Why are people so suspicious?

BETTY PAGE

Her hair is a black lake. Her hands are little white flowers growing out of her boneless arms, swaying in a breeze that always is where Betty is. Her legs are like those of a racehorse, big and strong enough for some real kicking. Even ball-gagged, stretched apart off the floor by rope and pulley, waist cinched by a rope, she's graceful, spirited, fun, beautiful, sexy and vibrant. She likes being bound up like that. Betty likes everything, 'cause she's on top of the world.

MY FRIEND RACHEL

She has C-cup breasts, but she still wears padded bras because she wants to make sure she always has the very biggest boobs in the room. Sometimes she sticks socks in her padded bra, saying one can never be too sure in a dicey world. Rachel practices extremism. However, Rachel believes her butt is too big. Foolish girl, no one's butt is too big. When I see a big butt walking around being kissed all over by tight pants or a tight skirt, I am filled with admiration. I think a big butt is very healthy, as well as useful—you have to have something to sit on; you don't want to sit on a couple of old bones.

If you look at evolution, we started out as monkeys with skinny little butts; then, as ape-men, got a little meat on our coccyx bones; then, as women (the apex of humankind's development) we grew nice, shiny, bulbous rear ends. Don't let your exercise bike catapult us back to the days of the buttless monkeys!

BANK TELLERS

They're so efficient. I can just picture them in the morning stepping into a lacy, good-smelling slip after the panties and hose, before the perfectly fitted, dry-clean-only skirt, unscuffed heels and hopelessly out-of-fashion yet irreproachably neat blouse, complete with bow.

Tell the truth—haven't you had impure thoughts about the bank teller?

LEFT EYE FROM TLC

I believe TLC originated that trend in video where the performers are wearing silk pajamas fifteen sizes too big and a big breeze just happens to be blowing the pajamas all over the place so you can see most of their skin anyway. It's an attractive fashion, but difficult to emulate in real life unless you carry a huge fan around with you. Anyway, my favorite member is Left Eye. She looks like a ten-year-old who'd play so many pranks she'd go through governesses like normal people use Kleenex. She set fire to her boyfriend's house, and do you know what happened to her? He gave her a million dollars! (He's a professional football player.) You can't help it—you have to love her. Her face is so cute and harmless, but I know she's dangerous. If I ever met her, who knows *what* she'd do to me? She likes to wear overalls and she can walk on her hands. She used to wear a monocle with a condom between it and her eye (the condom was still in the package). That is an odd fashion. She's a little spitfire.

T-Boz, the lead singer of TLC, is really, *really* tough. I'm afraid she's going to be mad that I didn't pick her as my favorite member and come find me and beat me up!

ROSEANNE

She looks great. Everyone made fun of her when she wore that red leather outfit. What, she's robust of flesh and so she can't be sexy if she wants? I bet she's fun in bed. She's really funny, but she can also get really dour and vile—like when talking about teen hookers: "It's our responsibility in Hollywood to stop glamorizing 'bad girls.'" God forbid!

She used to have the biggest cheeks you ever saw, but then got plastic surgery to turn them into two mean little ledges sticking out under her eyes. The old cheeks were so bountiful and inviting. Whenever I look at her now, I can't stop wondering about those cheekbones. Are they bones? If so, whose? Or are they plastic? The idea of plastic surgery appeals to me—creating oneself by force, playing a trick on fate. But the actuality scares me. The process of sawing parts off, or sticking artificial items in, seems so gruesome. It calls to mind space aliens abducting people and slipping a transmitter under their skin.

I realize this is not a popular view, but I find self-mutilation as compelling as it is revolting. I feel so powerful and flattered by the cruel things a woman does to herself—dieting, surgery, colored contact lenses that itch and cost a lot. It's not the things she does in particular. Most plastic surgery is actually kind of horrifying to look at, most dieting produces results not to my taste. It's that it seems like she did so much to herself for *me*, the person who spots her on the street or on TV. And then it's somehow endearing when they lie

about it: "No, I did not get an eye lift." It's that combination of ambition and awkwardness, like in seventh grade when I boldly put not
one but three pairs of socks in my bra and then, when I was found
out, burst into tears, denying it to the very end.

Glamour is not for the lazy or the satisfied. It's for the obsessed,
the unnaturally ambitious, the ones too bossy to listen when nature
tells them what to be. My kind of people!

In Favor

of Underwear

$\mathcal{I}$f you're like me, you spend more on your underwear than the entire rest of your outfit. It feels so decadent to blow all your money on something 99.9 percent of the population is never going to know about. Panties are one of very few secrets in life. If you buy a mahogany bed, you know your dinner guests will see it. If you get breast implants, everyone's gonna know. But, depending on your activity level, only one human at a time besides yourself is going to know what you have on between your legs.

Some girls think they're really sexy when they wear a skirt with nothing on underneath. To me, that's like serving a scoop of ice cream with no hot fudge and whipped cream topping. I'll take my sexual parts with all the trimmings, thanks.

In fact, I'm in favor of ladies in two or even three pairs of panties at a time. Oo-la-la, there's nothing sexier than peeling off a woman's panties to find . . . more panties! As for you men—don't bother putting on two pairs of your underwear. Men's underwear, like every other article of male clothing, is just not terribly appealing, and we don't want to see any more of those faded, most likely soiled drawers than we have to. There's nothing for men to do except work on their personality—the looks department is a lost cause. Men's bones come out at weird places; their curves aren't nice; they're hairy, and the hair is matted, or worn away in myriad unsymmetrical patches. They don't smell like us. A woman looks like a grown-up little girl. A man . . . I don't know what he looks like, but it's certainly not anything like how he started out. Some uncategorizable creature. Basically, men, you look like creeps. I have no idea why I'm so attracted to you.

Panties are surprisingly powerful for being such little things. A serious discussion—of Canada's medical insurance system or why something I did was wrong—is immediately forgotten when a peek of undergarments is presented. I feel I have lots of deep thoughts and enjoy intellectual conversations, but enjoy ending them even better.

There are many kinds of underwear. Furry ones, leather ones, ones with zippers or (God forbid) jokes written across the front, scented ones, but my favorites are the ones so delicate they look like they almost don't exist. Fabric laying gently between thighs like sea foam left behind after a wave, right before it evaporates into air. White lace with little, palest of pale blue hand-sewn lace flowers; clusters of baby pearls form the centers of the flowers. Right here is the apex of manmade beauty, like the peak of the most beautiful mountain. Streaming down the legs like pretty rivulets of ice and snow are the lines of the garters and the stockings—made of almost no color, they sparkle like face powder, and fascinate.

For a big change of pace, it might be racy to wear those old-lady cotton undies that go clear up to one's boobs. Only if the wearer is not really an old lady, though. (I've never tried it, but suddenly I know I must rush over to K-mart soon as I'm done writing, and pick up a pair and live out this rather staid fantasy.) Such chasteness at the door of such a hot treasurebox would make me, were I a man, feel like a real conqueror using one of those monstrous logs to ram down the heavy castle door. And he just hopes he won't fall prey to the alligators in the moat (the young girl's parents snoozing downstairs?). The danger is enticing.

One pair of these sturdy drawers, however, would be enough. It's too much to expect a man to ram down a heavy wooden door (or pull down thick cotton unders) every night. Sometimes a fellow needs to be invited in. Slithery French and feather panties are the trap doors in the castle no man can escape falling through. Life is treacherous, but rewarding.

Kissing

I've kissed three Frenchmen and a Belgian, but it just so happened that these kisses all occurred so late in the night it was actually the next day, and it also just so happened that alcohol was involved in each of the kisses, too—those Europeans, always staying up late and hitting the bottle (and influencing sweet and gullible Americans like me to do the same). It's a wonder they've managed to produce as many inventions as they have. Anyway, due to having been so tired and tipsy while kissing those foreigners, I cannot recall at all what it was like.

I wish I were much more of an expert on foreign kisses. I wonder, are the Japanese fast and rigid and formal and successful at kissing like they are at everything else? Are Russian kisses really long and dull like a Chekhov play? Are Chinese kisses short and multitudinous like the people? Do Middle Easterners succumb to religious fervor while kissing? When it's over, does the lady feel like jihad has been committed on her teeth and lips? Does she feel like she'll never bite an apple again? I'd like to know! I keep planning to go kiss some foreigners, but always end up kissing Americans over and over instead.

I really do have a thing about Japanese men. I think I'm the only one who does. They're so good at math! I want them to figure equations very promptly on the roof of my mouth. I want to be whisked away to a secret Asian lair where my Japanese man will spy on my mouth with his. He'll be looking for national secrets in there. Then he'll be gone before I can even figure out what happened to me. I'll be like, "What was that!" I won't even be sure I've been kissed. I have absolutely no idea why this scenario appeals to me, but

I've found it's better not to argue with my desires; they always win in the end.

But how will I get close enough to a Japanese man to get a kiss? There aren't any here in New Hampshire. To make my goal even more difficult to achieve, my *ideal* ideal is to be skillfully manipulated in the embrace of a fifteenth-century Japanese warlord with blackened teeth (that was considered sexy back then) in one of those rooms with parchment walls and no furniture. I guess I'll have to settle for lurking around the college campus, hoping a Japanese exchange student will scuttle off with me to his dorm room.

I bet Russian kisses *are* long and dull, no matter what century. Have you ever seen one of their movies? I once sat through a four-hour Russian movie where NOTHING HAPPENED. It was about nuclear disaster. I never knew disaster could be so boring. About a year later, I don't know what possessed me, I went to go see AN-OTHER Russian movie—this one was about nuclear disaster, too—and it was *even* LONGER, and EVEN LESS HAPPENED. I couldn't believe it. I think I would expire in a wintry Russian kiss that never ends.

Ki∧∧ing has very different meanings for men and women. For men it simply signifies that sooner or later (hopefully in five minutes) you're gonna have sex. For women it's a wild jamboree, a long and meaningful conversation of two souls, a chance to show off. I don't feel that way myself (I agree with the men), but that's how the women I've kissed act.

Women are mouth acrobats. They have to vary speeds and depth, do all these techniques—lick a person's teeth and vibrate their tongue against the flesh on the inside of the upper lips, and they're just really sophisticated. You're supposed to make your tongue long and skinny and entwine it with theirs. Women kiss in similes—their tongue is like a darting little lizard or a helicopter blade or a scared rabbit looking for a hole to jump down. I feel like I'm being experimented on. Women will call anything more than a peck on the cheek "a session." Despite all this, I still really like the ladies.

Men are more matter-of-fact about it. Some of 'em will just stick their big huge tongue all the way in your mouth with absolutely no finesse, like they're depositing a frog in there. (I must admit I kind of like that.) I like not being subjected to an anatomy lesson—I don't even want to know what he's doing. I just wanna ride a rocketship to Planet Instinct. On Planet Instinct you don't know anything. There are no houses on Planet Instinct; there's just one giant tornado and it attacks all visitors. When you're in a tornado, you don't have time to say yes or no to anything—you just spin. I want my lips to be murdered and then my tongue will resurrect like a Phoenix from the ashes of my demolished mouth . . . again and again and again! Oh, I don't feel that's too much to ask. It's just normal, when you're a prisoner on Planet Instinct. I believe that my mouth is a little bunny and there's a pack of vicious wolves out there—I want to meet them all! Then again, have you ever seen a bunny's teeth? The outcome of our rendezvous might be surprising. Perhaps when it's all over, the bunny will be wearing a wolf's-tail necklace under the smiling moon.

In conclusion, kissing with a man is wet, germy, hot and has very little to do with the mouth part of the body. Instead, it has everything to do with the parts down below. Like one's toes.

Once in a while there comes along a man who's a "good kisser." I'm afraid of those men. The kissee is supposed to be so overwhelmed by his learned maneuverings. It's a lot of pressure—like mirrors above the bed or riding in a Maserati or whatever car it is that's supposed to enrapture the ladies and costs a billion dollars. Kisses like that remind me of those hyperorganized tasks certain people are always doing that leave me dumbfounded—like winterizing the lawn mower. A fancy male kisser once accused me of not kissing with "soul." Whatever that means! Is soul like a *really slow* helicopter in the mouth? Do I have to kiss to the beat? Does soul mean exploring each crevice of all thirty-two teeth? My goodness, people do complicate their lives.

My first kiss was in fourth grade. It was with this really cute, greasy-haired, short kid named Mike. At the appointed hour, on Fifth Street by a fire hydrant, Mike and I held our four hands together and when I saw his face coming at mine I opened my mouth as wide as I could. (I thought I was being sensual.) Mike was startled. My first kiss ended a half a second after it began, and I didn't get another one for four years. I found out later Mike only kissed me because this big guy friend of mine threatened to beat him up if he didn't!

I wonder what the last kiss of my life will be like? The Ouija board says I'll live to be 80, and I usually go out with guys twice my age, so my boyfriend will be about 160. We probably won't have any teeth, or any lips either (take a close look at a really old person— their lips recede further and further into their mouth until there's nothing left but a line separating some wrinkled flesh from some other wrinkled flesh). We'll both most likely be blind, making us focus more on the sense of touch. I'm on my deathbed and we lean toward each other ever so slowly, our brittle bones creaking, our degenerating muscles aching. With my last bit of life I tenderly respond to his rotting, cancerous tongue's weak pokes . . . pain slows our movements even more, and I realize, "My God, I'm finally kissing with soul!" Then I die.

I know that in heaven Blackbeard the pirate waits for me. I shoot through the afterlife like I'm tobogganing down that tunnel at Waterworld. I'll be wearing a bikini in heaven—why not? At the end of the tunnel I drop onto the deck of Blackbeard's ship. The wind howls, the saltwater spray stings my eyes, and flotsam and jetsam expelled by the violent sea smash into me as that fiend Blackbeard presses his lips against mine with nary a word. It's daytime, but a black cloud obscures the sun. Blackbeard's hook presses into the small of my back, forcing me against his smelly old pirate body. His cutlass swings forward to tickle my right thigh, his pistol informs my other thigh of its presence. A magnificent beard scratches my neck and chest. I like it! Blackbeard pulls back and lets out a roar— me, too! When the storm is over, Blackbeard directs his men to row the ship onto land. It is a pirates' isle. Groups of men in ragged clothes and brilliant jewels count their gold coins, laugh into their beards, eat things that make their lips greasy and get into fights during which a lot of grunting goes on. Blackbeard throws a shovel at me and directs me to get digging. (For that is what pirates do— make their victims dig their own graves!) The sun beats down on my back as I dig all day, turning me red as a lobster. From time to time I look up at the seagulls careening high above and imagine I am one of them. (Why is this happening to me in heaven? Well, 'cause I like a bit of hard work, I love the beach and the pirates are cute, even if they are making me dig a grave.) When twilight turns the sand purple, my grave is done. Blackbeard pushes me into it, but my falling ankle catches his, and he tumbles down after me. There in the bottom of the cool, soft sand grave we finish our kiss, for all of eternity.

Now *there's* a kiss!

The World's Sexiest Devils: Russian Leaders

Soviet leaders are at either end of the continuum—either they're incredibly gray and bureaucratic or they're incredibly passionate and evil and animalistic and they go around threatening to rape women and stuff.

—*Pagan Kennedy*

*L*ike most Americans, I know very little about what's going on in the world. I can't seem to figure out politics or the masses or anything of that nature. 'Cause when I watch the news, my thoughts generally drift to how a date with the subject would go, and I forget to listen to the facts. Some people might fantasize about dating the local anchorperson, but I'm more ambitious: I imagine kissing Russian leaders.

I know I said I imagine their kisses are long and wintry, but sometimes that's exactly what one's in the mood for. Besides, who knows what combustion might result from the impact of my scalding-instant-coffee-gulping American lips upon frozen vodka-drinking, beard-covered Russian lips? Plus there's tragedy of some form in everything Russian, and tragedy is romantic. I like there to be a doomed quality to romance—a hopeless rebellion against fate makes me feel so young and reckless. It's supposed to be patriotic to despise communists, but I don't think of those people like that. I think about what we have in common—for instance, Russians like our Snickers bars, and so do I. Also, Russian men have lips, and so do I.

Russian history in the last two decades of the twentieth century will forever be entwined with mine: It just so happens that every Russian takeover correlated to some new stage of sexual maturation for me. It all started with Mikhail Gorbachev.

Author Gail Sheehy excited the young me by describing Gorbachev as having "transformed the world, while hesitating at the brink of his own radical psychological transformation—one that would enable him to see to its completion the revolution he so thrillingly began." That's exactly what I, in my virginal state, wanted—someone who would so thrillingly start, but certainly not see to completion, my transformation. Sex-crazed though I was, it was still scary to think of actually going all the way. But I certainly had no objections to the beginning part!

I saw a picture of the Russian president feeding a squirrel out of his hand—kind, dear, gentle man, ears elongated with age, dressed in a long black woolen coat, he looked like a priest. He's the kind of man who would put his arms around you and say, "Don't worry about your mother's hospital bills. We'll work it out somehow." Just a nice, nice man. When he was kidnapped during a coup, I felt the desperate, almost maternal, self-sacrificing need to rescue him from the probably hairy hands of those abducting brutes he later generously described only as displaying "an unbelievable lack of politeness." I imagined myself flying to Russia, wearing the hardliner symbol (if there even is one—I'd have to figure that part out later), so as to fool everyone about my real mission. One of the kidnappers falls madly in love with me, and thus I am able to steal the key to Gorbachev's cell. Then, while the others sleep, I sneak him out. "Come to the beach," he whispers. "No one will think to look for us there." We tell each other our life stories as dawn casts its white-blue glow, making everything look like an ice palace. "You'd better go to the underground bunker now, Mikhail," I warn him. He turns to stare into my ice-sparkling eyes. "I feel so safe here with you, away from oppressive enemies," he says, "and yet, Lisa! I am not safe from my passions!" And he gives to me passionate yet discreet kisses. "I want you so," he groans, "but I couldn't bear to hurt you. Our love affair is ill-fated." And he tears his lips from mine, rips the Russian cross from around his neck, presses it into my palm, and flees. I am left with a gentle throbbing in my body, and all my parts intact.

A year or so later, along came Boris Yeltsin—the big bully—to steal the presidency from his friend Mikhail with no remorse whatsoever. A callous beast. A drunken brute. Hmm . . . just what my present state of mind and body called for. No more passionate yet discreet kisses for me—passionate, really passionate, kisses were the order of the day! I didn't want to be a virgin anymore. With every inch of my pelt, I wanted to sin. The newspaper headlines only fed my fever. "Yeltsin Crushes the Revolt with Assault on Parliament." That guy's always assaulting someone or other! No wonder they call him "The Bear." (*Do* they call him The Bear? Well, *I* do, at least.) He crushed Parliament in a "bloody ten-hour fight with a potent show of force that left Russia's parliament building battered and in flames" (or is that "inflamed"?). "Oh, Yeltsin!" I cry, flinging down the papers and sucking on one ink-smudged finger. I'm yelpin' for Yeltsin. I wouldn't be saving *him* from any kidnappers—he'd be kidnapping me! Kidnapping my love.

My fantasy love affair with Yeltsin wasn't intricate—no surroundings, no situation, nothing in the world but his remorseless lips crushing mine. He won't take no for an answer . . . he's thinking only of his own pleasure . . . he grabs what he wants, and what I want is to be grabbed—with wild abandon! I want to be sinned on.

But my flame for Boris Yeltsin was just too hot to survive. Plus, he started taking a lot of "vacations" when his country needed him; he seemed to be losing control. The newscasters speculated about health problems brought on by alcoholism. One day I woke up and realized the truth: my Yeltsin is an old lush with a red proboscis. I don't want my man ill and out of control. I want him healthy, strong, cheery. I want the new man in town. I want Vladimir Zhirinovsky!

Zhirinovsky is a lover *and* a fighter: he's the sophisticated brute. He graduated from two fancy colleges, speaks eight languages, poses practically nude, says he'll take back Alaska, and makes weird, awful, secretly stimulating jokes, such as he likes hearing his bodyguards torture people in the night. He loves his country. His past is a shadow. Where *did* he get his money? *Is* he a KGB spy sent to divide Russia's democratic leaders? Is it true he's a secret tool of the

Anti-Zionist League to break Soviet Jews into warring factions? Is his father Jewish? I like a man of mystery. Oh, shadowy Russian Father Figure! He has nice lips. I don't care if I like a bad man! It's not my fault. It's not like I'm going to vote for him.

He says he has never loved anyone but his mother. Not even his wife. Of course, female-kind takes that as a challenge. "Naturally he's never truly loved," we think, "he's never met me."

My dream date with Zhirinovsky begins with him giving a lecture. I gaze up with enraptured eyes. When it's the audience-comment time, I use one of the lines I have been considering to replace the old "Better Red than Dead" slogan to show him where I stand on the Russian question. I've considered "Better Slavic-Kissed than Capitalist" and "Better a Spree in My Thighs than Free Enterprise" but I am not sure if he'd fall for either of those lines. Besides, actually I'm fond of capitalism. Nevertheless, for reasons known only to him, he invites me to dinner after the lecture.

I know a date with Vladimir Volfovich would be happening because he's so merry. He always laughs at his own jokes, and so do I. I'd laugh at his joke, then my joke, then his. He's a man of action, too. People protest, he throws flowerpots at them. What actions would happen on our date, I wonder? We better not go to a restaurant—Z. yells at waiters, and I just can't abide by that. We'd have a fight! I'd protest, he'd throw a flowerpot at me. I'd dump the salad bowl on his head and that would set off a full-scale riot. All the waiters, frustrated from years of abuse, poke my date with forks, and Zhirinovsky's aides hurl salt and pepper shakers at the waiters' heads. I'm caught in the crossfire, horribly wounded. Zhirinovsky and I end up in the same ambulance. My sympathy aroused by the sight of blood beading out of his multiple fork wounds, I lift my oxygen mask away from my face and give a tender kiss to his forehead. Awakened from his coma by my kiss, Zhirinovsky leaps up and has his way with my mouth and throat until the four medics finally manage to tear him off me. "Get off me, you buffoons!" he cries out. "Can't you see that at last I have found love with someone other than my mother? Ah, her name is Lisa. Oh, Lisa, I have waited all my long and lonely life for you! Now I will tell you, you and no one else, anything you want to know——such as whether or not it's true that I am a secret tool of the Anti-Zionist League to break Soviet Jews into warring factions." In the hospital bathroom I notice he gave me a hickey necklace. I haven't had one of those since eleventh grade!

Well, maybe we should go to a restaurant after all.

A new Russian presidential election is coming on. Yes, the Falcon is swooping down on the Bear. But Yeltsin might hold on yet——look at his face; that man's a tank. I'll like whoever wins. But what if it's one of those crusty communists? They're so old and humorless. And how would that correspond to my sex life? Dark times may lie ahead.

The Menfolk

Get Abused

for a

Change . . .

and Discover

They Like It!—

The Bee Gees

*f*or the baby boomers, The Beatles were the be-all and end-all musically, and boomers are so solipsistic they think it's that way for the rest of us, too. But for my generation, it was the lovely and tragic strains of the Bee Gees (and their fellow Australian, Olivia Newton-John) that molded our young, forming thoughts about love, life and what to do once we put on our boogie shoes. My generation is not solipsistic in the least—just the opposite. Each of us imagines we're the most alienated person on earth. Unfortunately for the Bee Gees, our big characteristic is irony, so we are forced to disavow the men who once moved us. And so, purely by cruel chance in the timeline of life, the poor Bee Gees are left completely unappreciated.

I know some people like the *Saturday Night Fever* soundtrack because they think it's campy, but the Bee Gees deserve respect as romantic, masochistic poet-geniuses with real spirit.

There is a twine of emotional and physical torture running through almost every Bee Gees song and the Brothers are *always* on the receiving end. That's because they're loyal in an unloyal world. Plus I believe they sort of enjoy it. What do you expect when you go around always singing lines like "you're so good treating me so cruel" and "no matter how you hurt me, I will love you till I die"? There are a lot of viperesses out there with hearts thin as razors to whom those lines are as alluring as the cry of a vole with a broken leg lying helpless on the desert floor . . . or whatever it is that snakes eat. Like the viperesses, I'm drawn, too. The Bee Gees cause a reverie in me.

Young Andy Gibb learned from his older brothers about hurts-so-good. He sings, "Shadow dancing, drag me across the floor." Ooh, his voice is so *dirty*. "Dra-a-ag me across the floor, uh-huh." Oh, my. The handsomest of the brothers, he unfortunately took the tragic elements of the Gibb makeup too seriously, and expired under mysterious circumstances at the age of thirty. The rumor is he died from a broken heart. That viperess Victoria Principal did it to him.

The Bee Gees really understood twentieth-century melancholia: "When you lose control and you got no soul." That's life in the city. The phrase "you're going nowhere" comes up in two songs—in one, they actually call out for someone to "help me, somebody help me there (nowhere)." They ask themselves, "Whatcha doin' there layin' on your back?" You know what these brothers are doing there—getting abused. Then they give themselves a pep talk: "You should be dancing, yeah." This struggle for optimism is what separates the boys—like Ian Curtis or Kurt Cobain—from the men. The Brothers' lively harmonies keep the despair from sinking into sludge. Early Bee Gees songs are so morbid and haunting—all about dying slow, horrible deaths . . . and they became top-40 hits!! My favorites are the one about the trapped miner suffocating, and that incredible paranoid one that goes: "Then I finally died / which started the whole world living / Oh if I'd only seen / that the joke was on me." When the Brothers moved into the disco era, the horror wasn't as overt—but that was just because you couldn't really tell what they were saying. I mean, the song "Tragedy" is all about tragedy, for God's sake . . . and it's cheerful. They're glad about their heartache, they celebrate it. In "Nobody Gets Too Much Heaven No More," a song about getting older and receding horizons, the brothers are disillusioned, but again, they keep the beat. They realize the world can be a very sad place but they don't forget they're singers and entertainers . . . they're dancing men!

Another feature of this supergroup is their fantastic imagery, mostly references to the four elements. I like it when people talk about the weather. I worked at Dunkin' Donuts from age fourteen to seventeen, and people talked about the weather there every day, and I never got tired of it. The Bee Gees talk about nature a lot, and they're really deep and dramatic about it. "I am your hurricane, your fire in the sun." *I* want a boyfriend who is a hurricane, a fire in the sun! He'd be uncontrollable. He'd be burning up. (At first I heard it as "I am your hurry king." I might like having a hurry king rushing me around, too. Maybe.) "Night and day is burning down inside of me," the Brothers say with an edge of desperation to their voices. It sounds wild! I imagine a solitary man moving with the wind down an emptied city street, swallowing all the power and magic of the enormous sky. My favorite song is the one where they say they want to take me where the eagles flow, where the rainbow ends. Oh, I do want to go where the eagles flow! I want some beautiful love.

Two nineties groups who, like the Bee Gees, sing about women leaving them and the weather are Hootie & The Blowfish and Boyz II Men. (One group who spell their name a stupid way and the other whose very name is just so stupid I can't even bring myself to say it out loud.) That puffy Hootie is so self-satisfied! I can totally picture him being all smug and thinking, "Ah, I understand the woman. Leaning against a lamppost in my plain old plaid shirt, I wait for her bad mood to pass and then I welcome her back like a sunrise and I hold her hand. Aren't I an admirable and sensitive boyfriend?" As for Boyz II Men—I can't tell at all what's behind all that intense warbling, and after watching their videos, I don't want to know. A popular one is where they're in a freezing downpour but instead of just going inside like normal human beings, they keep on singing even though they're probably gonna catch pneumonia. That's to show how extremely sincere they are. Then, when they finally do go inside, it's to gaze at a portrait they've painted of their ladyfriend and sing to it that they're sorry for some bad thing they did. That's laying it on a bit thick, don't you think? And you can't escape them—always quavering and clutching their hands, doing duets with everybody, so there'll be eight Boyz-related songs in a row on the radio. Boyz are *everywhere.*

I feel so bitter that these Hooties and Boyz, in their "sincere" clothes and lovesick puppy faces, are revered and my Bee Gees are made fun of or forgotten. Sometimes I feel like I can't bear to live in a world where the Hooties and Boyz reign. Then I force myself to change the channel, and news of a millionaire murdering a bright-purple-and-green-attired wrestler pleasantly distracts me.

The only nineties performer I see worthy of wearing the Bee Gees mantle of grandiose love hurried on by an eternal wind is Seal. Seal informs the lady that she is "the light on the dark side of me." He goes on: "And did you know that when it snows my eyes become enlarged and the light that you shine can't be seen?" Well, no, I didn't know that. As with the Bee Gees, I'm not sure what Seal is trying to say, but it sounds so traumatic and interesting that I immediately imagine the song is about me. "You remain my power, my pleasure, my pain," Seal is telling me. I like to be talked to like that! I can't wait for his next album to come out so I can find out what else I am.

On the one hand, Seal has a great body and compares me to a kiss from a rose on a grave; on the other hand, Seal doesn't have any brothers, and does have pits in his cheeks that I hear he claims are "scarification" he did himself in African or Australian aboriginal fashion, but I have my suspicions. Due to these minor infractions, my heart still belongs to the Bee Gees.

I never seriously considered, like I did with just about every other group, which one of the Brothers Gibb I'd like most to be my true love. They seemed more like voices than human beings. Pure, disembodied angelic voices—breezes weaving through ornate melodies, like the rain, the wind, the night and the sky that they compare to love in every single song. (One woman comes to them on a summer breeze, another came on like the night.) Listening to them is like riding an escalator to ecstasy, every time. When I looked at their poster, I knew one was named Barry, but wasn't sure which one. To me they were Hairy, Fairly Hairy and Baldy. Poor Baldy—he's so sincere. (I mean really sincere, not that fake, boastful Hootie sincerity.)

But these angel men have a dark side, too! How their blatant sexual references got past all censors and became number-one hits, I'll never know. I swear to God the chorus of one song is "Sodomy! Sodomy!" Another song goes: "Fanny be tender with my love / you know how easy it is to hurt me." *Fanny?* Another voice comes on to order: "Squeeze into yourself, boy." I don't know *exactly* what that means, but I do know it sure is dirty.

I won't forget what you taught me, Bee Gees. You taught me to identify wind blowing across the field as a messenger of a grand love waiting for me somewhere out there, to feel raindrops on my face as bittersweet kisses from a faraway lover. You taught me to dance. You taught me to smile through my pain. In fact, you taught me to really enjoy my pain! I love you, Bee Gees.

Attention K-mart Shoppers: A Loving Tribute to a Dying Friend

*T*he K-mart parking lot is monstrously large, busy and not too artistic. There's a real feeling of purpose, and a hint of danger, as you slam your car door and stride that long way to the six huge front doors, darting to the left and the right to avoid improperly supervised children, carts rolling free and predatory cars searching out that perfect space right near the entrance.

K-mart is great. All that *stuff* strewn around aisle after air-conditioned aisle, and the Muzak versions of Culture Club and Madonna songs make you really feel like you're shopping. Don't be daunted by the piles of voluminous clothing in bright, ugly colors. With a little patience the prizes—like a bandana halter top or a tight black shirt with a big plastic orange butterfly over the boobs— can be yours . . . for $1.99 each!!! The problem most people have with K-mart clothes is they're cheaply made and behind the times, but that's no problem for me! Some of my best friends are cheaply made and behind the times.

The difference between K-mart and all the other marts is K-mart is cheap and gaudy, while the others are just cheap. Take the Angel Bubbles Barbie I saw at K-mart one time—maybe not the most craftsmanship or finesse went into this doll, but she's an angel and bubbles come out of her. I think that's pretty fancy! I'm in favor of gaudiness for the poor. If you're Kelly Klein and you have a tanning salon in your house and a personal trainer to help with your "problem areas," and you can go to a spa or a plastic surgeon for glowing, happy skin whenever you want, then you look good in just a plain brown shirt and jeans. When you're a K-mart shopper, that's not a "problem area"—that's your butt. When your skin is sallow nine months a year and you have crow's feet and you drink too much, your appearance can only benefit by having feather earrings and a big bubble-plastic butterfly on your chest. You gotta have some bravado. You gotta distract people; they'll be so fascinated by the glitzy elements of your wardrobe they won't even notice your physical faults and poverty. So what if the stitches at the seams aren't so tight? What do I care if my clothes fall apart after twenty wearings? I don't want to wear the same thing a million times anyway. And if I really love something, I'll buy three of it—that way I can be seen in it sixty times. And I've still paid only six dollars! As for not being fashionable: I think it's cute to be six months to two years (or more!) behind everybody else. So some gal might look at you in your tight K-mart jumpsuit (pink, with matching pink bubblegum popping in and out of your pink glossy lips) and think, "God, that outfit is so 1982! And there's a thread unraveling—can't she afford anything better?!" But that mean gal's boyfriend is thinking, "That looks good!" He might even think, "Hmm, I sure would like to yank on that loose thread and see what happens." Men don't know or care what's in style. The K-mart shopper knows clothes are to be worn for two reasons: to keep you from getting sunburn, and to make those of the opposite sex wonder what you look like without 'em. You don't need to spend a bunch of money or buy *Mirabella* to check out the "new fall line" in order to accomplish either of those aims. It's impossible to keep up with couture so why try? Nobody notices except for frigid snobs anyway, and you don't want to hang around them. I don't care for that bitchy competitiveness that is rooted in absolutely no reality (I'm talking about fashion).

There are two types of K-mart shoppers: loud, skinny, rug-ratty ones who like to farm their offspring off to various relatives so they can stop in the makeup aisle and dot cheap perfume behind their ears and then flirt with the male manager; and pear-shaped, lumpy ones, quieter than the skinny ones, softer, with several children, and occasionally a potato-shaped husband, in tow. Of course, thrill-seeker that I am, I prefer the former—but it's lucky for the cause of peace that the majority of shoppers are the latter. Get too many of those rug-ratty types together and there's sure to be a riot! There was always a certain time to most fear them: when the blue-light special would be announced over the intercom, that uninhibited, predatory, cussing beast stalking the aisles of K-mart would go mad, shoving her way to the racks of work pants or the shelves of multi-opening photo frames, even if she didn't need whatever item was on sale. I like excitable people. And if all this tussling gets you hungry, you can have a hot dog, pizza, soft pretzel and soft-serve ice cream at the gay red-and-white-striped food corner of K-mart. You can even have your photo taken so that it looks like you're in a beautiful wood scene or your face is floating in a champagne glass—and you get one hundred copies for only $1.95! What a deal! And as you wait in line to pay for your purchases, there are astrology scrolls and all sorts of informative booklets to read (the K-mart shopper likes to be in-formed): "How to Talk to Your Cat": "Do Angels Exist?"; "Baby Names"; "Top Secret Word Search"; and "Home Remedies from the Bible" (What could those be? "If thy hath insomnia, hurl thineself into a Pit of swarming snakes"?); and "Banish That Belly." You won't need to waste your thirty-nine cents on that last booklet—you've already banished that belly evading all those carts the fierce ladies wield as weapons.

The last few years, there's been a real feeling of decline in the halls of K-mart. The shoppers are still feisty and wiry (except for the ones who are lumpy and determined), but it's like degenerative bone disease has afflicted all those who've been shopping there for more than a decade. They're haggard. A teacher-friend informed me that K-mart is now out and Wal-Mart is in. The kids make fun of K-mart—it's not cool, it's behind the times, depressing. If K-mart goes out of business, what's going to happen to the old-lady cashiers who've been with the company for forty years and haven't aged gracefully because they've been eating at the snack bar all this time?

Where will they go? It's really sad. Also, what will happen to me? My youth is tied up in K-mart. I learned to shoplift there. I got my first training bra there (white with little blue flowers; it wore out before I could outgrow it). I think I'm writing a happy little chapter about my favorite shopping experience and then I realize I'm delivering the eulogy. For the first time I see myself on the wrong side of young—the kids are shopping one place and I'm still haunting the aisles of what has become an uncool place. I'm one of the degenerative bone disease hags! But even as it falls apart, there's something noble about K-mart—or at least historical. Well, even if it's not noble or historical, at least it's old. It's like a big, lumbering dinosaur that doesn't know where to turn. It's being driven out of business by that quicker, craftier, cheaper chain store, Wal-Mart. Wal-Mart is gutting K-mart . . . with a grin on its putrid, well-scrubbed face. Every time I go to K-mart now, the shelves are barer and barer. Walking down its aisles, looking up at an ever more paltry selection, I feel like I'm inside the belly of a starving beast.

I visited Wal-Mart to see what all the fuss is about. That place is sinister. There's a hateful air in its low-ceilinged, narrow, cluttered, endless aisles. Items are stacked right up to the low ceilings. And half of the boxes are empty—why is that? A guy reached for a drill teetering at the very top of a pile of junk and it dropped on his head. He sued, and Wal-Mart had to pay him a million dollars. Good! I'm not normally in favor of suing over one's own stupidity, but anything bad that happens to Wal-Mart is right by me. At K-mart you can see different sections in the distance—there's a horizon; Wal-Mart is so crammed together you can't see past your own aisle. With all those families milling around, you start to feel feverish.

It says a lot about people's character whether they shop at K-mart or Wal-Mart—the latter shoppers don't have any. Everyone protests when a Wal-Mart comes to town because they deliberately put mom-and-pop stores out of business—yet the bulk of America shops there. It can't be good for one's soul to shop where you know you shouldn't. Maybe the shoppers are former protesters who feel guilty and since nobody wants to feel that way, they close down their soul. Maybe that's why Wal-Mart shoppers are rude and greedy and the salespeople are zombies. Yeah, they can be rude at K-mart, too, but at least they express their nastiness in a lively way. I'd rather get a dirty look than a blank one. Some K-mart shoppers are in their own world, gazing dreamily at their favorite sheer nightie; some are rude and rushing, but they do it with glee. Wal-Mart shoppers are never dreamers and they're never gleeful. They're just smug because they think they're middle class. I got news for them—if you're middle class, you shop at Pier One, not Wal-Mart. I don't even like the way the word *Wal-Mart* looks.

Maybe I'm just reacting emotionally here—maybe Wal-Mart's problems and K-mart's superiority are all figments of my imagination. But I don't care! I don't care if I have to spend eight cents more per item to shop at K-mart—I'll go on doing it till the very last day. I can't believe K-mart's time is almost gone. K-mart is the fertile American field that has yielded that gum-smacking, uninhibited, wildly cheerful (though sometimes in a rather violent way), bargain-hunting beast. Down its glowing fluorescent aisles, charging and lunging and shoving, the shoppers are like dry stalks of corn waving madly in the American wind.

The Rat Fink and Princess Horsie

I **believe** the most beautiful sight on earth is a figure skater. I can't understand how they create such beauty from nothing but moving around in a circle in a big cold room. My heart feels like a bird when I see them. I feel noble just for having witnessed such a thing.

Figure skating is not ornate. It's nothing like the Sistine Chapel or Liberace. It's only movement. Just that. And the skaters have to work so hard to achieve their purity; training ten hours a day from childhood on, a trainer mercilessly pointing out the tiniest flaws and ordering, "Do it again."

"But Natassia," the nine-year-old peeps out, "it's so late and I'm ever so tired. Please can't I do it tomorrow?"

Natassia fixes a beady eye on the sixty-nine-pound girl shivering before her—the eye of the owl on the rodent—and answers with a low but deadly, "Do it."

Tears form like diamonds in the eyes of the poor little skater. She sadly pushes away from the side of the rink to the center, where she flawlessly executes a triple axle, ice flying from her blades like sparks.

These people are not normal. It's not normal, I tell you, to be so dedicated and single-minded practically from infancy. So it makes sense that the ingredient in their psyche that motivates them to create such extreme beauty also causes just plain extremeness. Hockey players skate around on ice as a career, too, but you don't see *them* marrying each other and then dying of a heart attack in their wife's arms right there on the ice, or cavorting about dressed as a nymphetic Catholic schoolgirl with a big lollipop (Oksana Baiul's latest routine).

Figure skating is probably best known now for the incident involving Nancy Kerrigan, Tonya Harding and a stick. At the time that it was big news I didn't really care about it, because both ladies' faces were just so repulsive. One looked like a horse, the other a rat. And both were whiners.

Only later did I realize this series of events was in fact a dramatic illustration of the war of the classes. I also started seeing myself in Tonya. I, too, resemble a rodent—though I'm fortunate in that my face calls to mind the cute gerbil and not the hated rat. Nancy Kerrigan represented all the privileged "Barbies" who snubbed gerbil-faced me in high school.

While all the other skaters, including Nancy Kerrigan, look like dolls and grew up in pretty houses, Tonya Harding grew up among the strip malls and trailer parks in Beaverton, Oregon, where there's nothing to do but drive into Portland or shop at Target and smoke a lot of pot. Tonya has close-set eyes, thunderthighs, and looks dumpy no matter what she wears. She appears to be a midget, though she is not one. God did not intend for Tonya Harding to be a skater, but our Tonya didn't let that stop her for one second. Nancy Kerrigan comes from a genteel background—she had braces and everything. Her parents were dedicated; they took her to the best rinks. Tonya didn't get along with her mother or any of her mother's six husbands, so she put all her energies into skating, even if she had to skate on a pond in April when the ice was breaking up and she might die! While Nancy's diamond-studded white dreamlike skating outfit cost $13,000, Tonya's hideous purple leotard didn't quite match her Lee Press-Ons. Princess Nancy Goody-Two-Shoes married a lawyer or her agent—some man who pays a lot for his haircuts—and everyone said how beautiful the wedding was; Tonya married some blue-collar worker who took porn movies on their honeymoon and later sold them to *A Current Affair*! She was only fifteen! The husband was kind of good-looking in a scary Freddie Mercury way—overbearing teeth forcing their way out beneath an overbearing mustache. Tonya kept getting restraining orders against him, but I guess she couldn't restrain herself from welcoming back that fiercely mustachioed fellow, because they never did split up for long. Even after Tonya sued for divorce (at the ripe old age of nineteen), those two maniacs couldn't keep out of each other's arms. The divorced couple moved into a cabin on a Christmas tree farm, having been evicted from their apartment for failing to pay rent. Of course, there are no stories to relate concerning the blissfully secure Kerrigans . . . not until Tonya and her mister smashed into their perfect life, that is.

Tonya and her sleazy husband and their goon friend were sitting around drinking beer one night and they decided they're going to have the goon go hammer Nancy Kerrigan's knee—in front of millions of witnesses, no less—since Nancy was Tonya's only real competition. This is the kind of stupid idea that occurs to people when they drink beer. I must admit that when I drink beer and start thinking about that woman's toothy smirk, and how she tosses around her luxurious dark mane that I'm sure she prides herself on every ten seconds—"It's so healthy! Oh, how jealous those with split ends from over-processing must be"—why, then I, too, get the desire to hammer her knee. Of course, I wouldn't *do* it. But these three *did*. And what consequences did Tonya suffer? Practically none. She has to do some community service, pay a fine, and she can't skate professionally anymore. Actually, she has embarked on quite an interesting life since then. Her career moves have included mowing lawns, being a pro-wrestling manager, acting, singing, plus the Japanese paid her a bunch of money to play Ping-Pong with one of their Ping-Pong stars. (If I weren't American, I'd wish I were Japanese. Those people are always doing weird things and paying people millions of dollars to do it with them.) The academic feminists deconstruct Tonya semiologically, making allusions to the ancient Greeks, and professional golfers are rumored to be stalking her. It's truly amazing: here's this young, ugly girl, with no charm, not much brains and oodles of ambition, who had somebody brutally *attacked*, and she didn't even go to jail but made money off it instead by doing all sorts of unusual things. Now that's a fine display of American opportunism. Tonya Harding can say "What the heck?" and jump feet first into something crazy. That quality counts for more than all the squalidness of the rest of her being.

Nancy Kerrigan went on to play the victim role for all it was worth, making a career out of appearing on the morning interview shows, saying, "Why me?" This is opportunistic, too, but not a fine display, for it utterly lacks spirit. She did all the normal, acceptable figure skater events. Then she was doing Disney On Ice for a New Year's Eve or Christmas parade and a mike inadvertently picked up her saying, while smiling and waving at the throngs of happy children at the foot of her float, "This is the lamest parade I've ever seen." People saw her then for the ungrateful, spoiled little somebody she truly is, boy, and she hasn't been heard from much since.

Everyone loves the horse because they've always seen her on puzzles and posters, her pelt shiny and smooth. And everyone hates the rat because it eats gross food and scurries around doing mysterious, possibly frightening things at night. Still, I'd rather be the rat. The rat goes where it wants—especially where it's not wanted—while the horse has to wear a saddle and stay in the stable. And I do enjoy gross food from time to time, and want to go do some of those mysterious, possibly frightening things at night myself! "Yes," I think when contemplating the distasteful, wizened face of Tonya Harding peering out from the pages of old *People*s at my doctor's office, "the rat is little but her bite is big."

A Nice Girl Mixed Up with the Wrong Crowd: Olivia Newton-John

Her voice is heavenly. It's ethereal. I was surrounded with so much reality. I felt strapped to the earth, and to my parents' home in particular. I followed her voice out. I felt like she was specifically talking to me. At the dinner table I would hear her songs note for note in my head, drowning out the yelling.

—*Cindy Dall*

*O*ut of all the dreams I had in my youth, Olivia Newton-John was the most beautiful one. Every morning when I woke up in the years 1980 and 1981, Miss Newton-John gazed serenely at me from her poster, light emanating from her head and a gentle breeze lifting her hair, promising me a limitless future.

The entire female half of my generation wanted to be like her—so pretty, so delicate, so nice, knowing how to do all those dances, knowing how to ride a horse. When Olivia permed her hair for the final scene of *Grease*, we all went out and did it, too. In the early 1980s, entire classrooms all across America looked like broccoli patches—skinny little bodies and big curly heads. "She just had this *power*," my friend Itchie describes, "I was so drawn to her. We all were."

Olivia was magic. She encompassed apparent contradictions without presenting them as such, allowing us to redefine our concepts. This is most evident in her movies, where she plays good girls who do bad things and no one minds. In *Grease* the major conflict is that Olivia's eighteen-year-old character, Sandy, won't have sex with John Travolta's bad boy character, Danny. In the end Sandy gets a perm and wears hoop earrings and tight black leather. She puts her hand on Danny's chest and pushes him through a rotating tunnel at an amusement park, telling him, "You're the one that I want!" The shocked but happy boy's answer, "I got chills, they're multiplying, and I'm losing control, 'cause the power you're supplying—it's electrifying!" is entirely understandable! Sandy is obviously going to have sex with Danny at the day's end, and the whole school is singing "dippety-dip-de-dip!" to celebrate. In *Grease*, "evil" (de-virginizing a 1950s good girl) wins out in the end. Surprising!

But Olivia is not simply a "good girl gone bad." She does "bad" things just as nicely as she does "good" things. In *Xanadu*, she asks a date to sneak her after dark into the control booth of the amusement park/studio that inspires recording artists. Delighted, she asks him to push all the buttons at once—get the whole thing going. He gets nervous because he doesn't know how to run the machine and worries that he'll break it. She just laughs and tells him to "push them all *gently* then!" There's no "we're breaking fucking society's rules, heh, heh" guilty pleasure here—Olivia's wearing the same innocent, shining smile she wore earlier while roller-skating legally in the park. In "Magic" she sings, "Nothing can stand in our way." There can always be a suspension of the rules or a loophole through them when Olivia's around. Breaking into the studio could wreck this guy's current life, yet Olivia is happy doing it, and she makes him happy. "Everything in Western culture is based on guilt and blame and obligation," my physicist friend told me. Olivia doesn't operate that way. She does what brings her and others pleasure and joy, and judges nothing and no one. Occasionally she's miserable, but that's always brought on by others' inept living. A lot of smarty-pants people like to talk about Nietzsche talking about "beyond good and evil." That's a lot of talking! These intellectuals would no doubt join that large group of people who scoff at Miss Newton-John as a "lightweight"—she who *is* beyond good and evil. Like her crystalline voice, Olivia Newton-John is absolutely pure.

But in the early nineties, we former broccoli sprouts realized we'd fallen short of our Olivia dream. She was the perfect role model, but we had to turn her down. We realized there was going to be no gentle breeze forever lifting *our* hair. The air of our life generally just sits there like a dumb, stubborn frog, but on rare occasion it whips into big gusts that break our umbrella and make us feel crazed like an Arabian horse with nostrils quivering, and that's gotta be better than any gentle breeze ever could be. To be Olivia-like, we'd have to be small and pretty, and it was hard to tell if we were pretty under all that eyeliner and those bangs, and when we grew up we turned out to be—well, *big.* Olivia wouldn't drink too much or talk mean to her boyfriend, but we did all the time. We were a little too sleazy, a little too forceful, a little too brunette to be Olivia. Plus we kept on falling down on our Rollerblades. So, in our tottering heels or our lawyerly loafers, we marched on into our slightly soiled future, and Olivia Newton-John floated behind as a sweet memory, along with Bubblicious bubble gum (twelve pieces in the mouth at once), sunbathing (we didn't care about wrinkles then—we figured once we got old—twenty-two or so—we might as well be ugly, too), and afternoons spent perfecting cheers, acrobatics or some other synchronized moves to be carried out by six or more females in front of crowds of parents and peers.

Eventually we discovered that even Olivia Newton-John is nothing like Olivia Newton-John. We thought she *was* the face in the poster, but in real life Olivia lost a breast to cancer, has the best home security system of the stars because there are so many kooks stalking her, and was part of a long-time menage-à-trois! (My friend Jaina assures me absolutely that last one is true.) These facts show Olivia the person as being not as magical or dreamlike wonderful as her celluloid image, but capable of doing something rented videos never can: getting hit by life—by tragedy, fear and weird sex—and finding out what happens next.

Her beautiful songs and movies remain an eternally open expressway to all the dreams we acrobatic broccolis left behind when we pressed forward into our real life and became bank tellers and welfare moms and bitter divorcées. Of course it's a little disappointing to realize you're never actually going to be a duchess—in fact, we're not even going to ever be the very nice, sweet person we thought we'd be, but it's so interesting to finally *be* rather than to dream, even if what you're being is a crabby overweight fishstick-box assembler in debt. That's *your* crabby-overweight-fishstick-box-assembler-in-debt life, and if there's gonna be a fight at the dinner table, no one can send you to your room. You can go on yelling as long as you want, and if you want to have sex with a bad man who's going nowhere, or eat sixteen Chunky bars in a row and no vegetables, no one can stop you! I'm certainly enjoying finding out what people and life beyond the Dover public school system and The Strand theater are really like instead of just imagining it all. I'm just grateful to Miss Newton-John for keeping in the notes of her songs the perfect memory of what it was like only to dream of the future that I now hold firmly in my doctor-dialing, diaper-changing, paycheck-blowing hands that I'm having a hard time keeping on the table. You know what I mean?

The Manifest Destiny of Anna Nicole Smith

*W*hen *seven-year-old* Jessica Dubrof died trying to be the youngest pilot to fly across the country, all these self-righteous men and disapproving women called up the radio stations to say how awful it was she was flying. I guess they think she should've stayed in her room. They feel seven-year-olds should be humble, and it's the parents' responsibility to strong-arm them into that humility. *U.S. News and World Report* censoriously suggests that Jessica's father somehow forced, or at least encouraged, her to act cheerful and brave, as if that was the epitome of evil parenting. The radio callers say she didn't get a chance to live her life. I got so mad I called up the radio and told them she *was* living her life, which is more than most people can say. There are some people who are born risk takers, willful and extravagant, and even their failures are greater than the greatest accomplishments of the people who stay in their room and never die in a plane crash. Our country was made great by having so many of those types, but now their existence just seems to make people mad.

America is divided today into offended citizens and citizens paralyzed with the fear of offending. Some unhappy souls are both at once. I hope this blight is temporary, because it just isn't natural. We're not that way! I wonder when it happened that offending someone became so terrible and special. Getting offended is part of life, like falling out of love or having to go to the bathroom really bad on a long car trip with no exits in sight. There's no cure for being offended, any more than there's a cure for life. All of a sudden, feeling offense is the surest guarantee to get what you want. This landlady was offended by those living in sin, and refused to rent to any. One rejected renter got on the news and said, "I was so offended!" So she sued the old lady right up to the Supreme Court, so they could decide who had the bigger right to feel offended. She was supposedly suing to force the landlady to rent to her and her boyfriend, but they didn't even want to live there anymore! She was just driven by offendedness.

I wish these people would get a grip. I don't even think of them as Americans—they're nothing like the wild ones who carved out this big country. Fear of offending—sometimes called "sensitivity"—has stopped the American from letting his or her naturally odd, lusty, lively personality flower. The biggest offense of all today seems to be being different. People take it as a personal attack. Anna Nicole Smith's breasts, being different from the average breasts, are taken as an open and deliberate insult. They're not the type of breasts to stay in their room and be humble. The way people treat those breasts in conversation, you'd think they were twin marauders breaking into houses and stealing the family jewels.

Anna Nicole is my hero. Her personality matches her larger-than-life figure. She's a real take-charge type of person; she wasn't born an heiress, so she made herself one. No one marries eighty-nine-year-olds anymore . . . no one but A.N.S. Anna Nicole is the only role model available to Dover youth too antsy to do data processing at the navy yard and too lacking in social skills to be a cosmetician. Stripper, heiress, addict, mother—most people can only manage one or two, or at most three, of those in their lifetime. Not our Anna—she can do all that at once, and more!

She has flair. She spent one million dollars a day on her husband's credit card until he died. I couldn't even spend a million dollars in my whole life! I get tired just walking around the mall trying to spend $200 on Christmas presents. Where does she get all her energy? She is so spectacularly American that Europeans are knocked senseless by her charms. Billboards of Anna Nicole had to be taken down in Germany because they were causing too many traffic accidents. See how powerful it can be when you let your national character really flower?

Like her home state of Texas (where she worked in a fried-chicken shop), which is on the bottom of the map, A.N.S. started out on the bottom of life. Everyone told her she was too fat to be a model, but she didn't care—she bleached her hair white-blonde, put on tight dresses, and became *Playboy* Pet of the Year and modeled Guess jeans. Then she landed a juicy role in *Naked Gun 33⅓*. She did very well at acting, I felt. She lit up the screen! The rest of the theater audience—a gaggle of eleven-year-old boys—felt the same way. I'm tired of every single woman in entertainment being "smart" and talking in interviews such in a smart and humble way. "How will you feel if you win the Golden Globe Award?" "Oh, I don't think about that, just to be nominated is such an honor. There are so many other talented actresses nominated, they all deserve the award." They think they're going to fool everyone into thinking they're sweet and down to earth, but actually it is very poor manners not to get excited about a gift. Sandra Bullock *refused* her nomination, claiming it should go to an actress with "a larger body of work." I think Miss Smith has quite a large body of work, and she should get nominated. Voracious Anna would say, "I want it! Give it to me! Give me that statue!"

I believe she and her husband loved each other. She claimed she liked his personality, and who am I to doubt her word? She also said he was "frisky." People thought Anna Nicole's lowcut funeral dress and the gold glitter and teddy bears with which she decorated the funeral parlor proved that she didn't really care about her husband and was using his death as a publicity event. (I did think wearing lipstick the color of caked blood was a little morbid, but then all the greatest glamour contains a touch of morbidity.) But gold glitter, teddy bears and lowcut dresses were exactly what made Howard (the husband) call Anna Nicole "the light of my life." There had been a lot of sadness in Howard's life—shortly after his first wife died of Alzheimer's, his girlfriend, "Jewel" the stripper, died while having cosmetic surgery. Anna Nicole, gaudy, cutesy, sexeee and nuts—what a bright creature to enter a sad man's life! Plus she'd do "booby dances" for him. That must've been fun. I think Anna Nicole is interesting. Her bodyguard accused her of sexually molesting him, then her female housekeeper did the same! An old man, a burly man and a dumpy housecleaner: Anna Nicole has surprising taste in sexual partners. I love to be surprised.

So Anna Nicole is not brilliant. Maybe she's brilliant when talking about certain things, or when doing her booby dance. It's not a crime to have a low IQ.

I remember reading somewhere that she takes ten hours to get ready each day. It's altruistic of her to always want to put on a good show—even when she's only going out for a magazine and a bagel. This willingness to go the extra mile to dazzle is what took this dumb, plump mother-of-one out of the chicken shop into superstardom—causing car wrecks in Germany and everything! Just imagine what my son's thirteen-year-old pretty but boring baby-sitter's life would be like if she took ten hours to get ready each day: she'd have to get up at nine o'clock at night in order to make it to school by seven-thirty. I'd be so impressed I'd give her a raise from $3.50 an hour to $5. She'd be so exhausted she would believe in her sleepless confusion that I'd molested her, and go down to the police station and accuse me. We'd be in the paper, and U.P.I. would run her photo. She'd be discovered and then she'd be in the next *Friday the 13th* movie and make *$500* an hour. With all that money she could have the piano lessons she'd always wanted, become a world-class pianist and marry a cellist. They'd tour in the symphony together and be so happy.

It's been a while since I've heard anything about Anna Nicole, and I fear that her popularity is waning. I want to be in charge of her comeback. I'll write a book about her called *Anna Nicole Smith: She Has Really Large Breasts.*

I admire Anna Nicole because she is living out the American dream: making the most of her God-given talents without a shred of guilt. Plus, she takes good care of her young son. She's tops!

In the lovely and ancient Dover cemetery on Central Avenue, where I once got caught by a policeman having sexual relations with my boyfriend, there's a funny gravestone—a statue of a weeping woman, Cordelia Teatherly, bitterly turning her back on the gravestone of a harness maker named Henry Law, who jilted her in 1861 because his dog didn't get along with her dog and she refused to part with her beloved pet. He left her at the altar when they were only twenty, and the fight between them lasted for seventy-six years until both were dead. A big fight! Even though both married others, they continued to say horrible things about each other and each other's dogs to all the relatives and to everyone else they knew. They played pranks on each other even fifty years after the event. It was a nasty, crazy, heated fight they just couldn't quit. A fight that, in stone over the bones, will last on into eternity, for all the ancestors to see. I like a good fight!

To be truly American, one must have lots of personality. It doesn't have to be a *good* personality; there just needs to be a lot of it. Cordelia Teatherly, Anna Nicole and Jessica Dubrof each embody, in their own way, the quality that made America, for better and for worse, what it is. None of the three were proper. All of them went beyond the boundaries. They had that most American of qualities: excess.

Americans aren't satisfied with just one or two murders—we have to have serial killers. Pretty models who walk well aren't enough for us—we have to have supermodels with anorexia *and* bulimia and billions of dollars. Our buildings can't just be nice and useful—we have to build skyscrapers bigger and bigger and bigger. We're just that way. We invented mass production because we had to have more. We invented fast food because we had to have it quicker. We have the most fat people in the world. We're *hungry.* We have the most intrusive mass media because we're nosy. We have to know, and we have to know now. We're also impulsive, eccentric and can't be fenced in. And I say long live the bountiful personality. Love live the people who make people mad. Long live the ones who won't listen to sense. Long live the people who are forever getting warned, "one of these times, you're going to go *too* far!" Long live the fiery, the unguilty, the unhumble, the dazzling, the cheerful and the brave. Even if they don't live long, even if they look obnoxious or even stupid in a certain light, they're still wonderful and magnificent to me, and they're free, free, free.